J.W. Thomas

Star-Beams

J.W. Thomas

Star-Beams

ISBN/EAN: 9783337410278

Printed in Europe, USA, Canada, Australia, Japan

Cover: Foto ©Andreas Hilbeck / pixelio.de

More available books at **www.hansebooks.com**

STAR-BEAMS;

OR,

RAYS OF LIGHT.

BY

J. W. THOMAS.

"I am the bright and morning star."—JESUS.

"They that be wise shall shine as the brightness of the firmament, and they that turn many to righteousness as the stars forever and ever."—DANIEL.

PROVIDENCE:
ANGELL, BURLINGAME & CO., PRINTERS.
1875.

PREFACE.

This volume is not sent forth into the world presuming to give the light of the sun or of the moon, but in comparison with many other volumes only the light of a little star; hence the author has given it the modest title of Star-Beams or Rays of Light.

Some good thoughts have been selected, but it is composed mostly of original articles, a portion of which have before appeared in various religious periodicals during several years past. The acceptance with which they have met, and the encouragement which has been received from editors and from friends in different parts of the country, has led to their publication in the present form, that they may be more permanently preserved, and if possible more extensively circulated. If through the perusal of these pages, some sinner shall behold a ray of light, and be guided into the pathway of righteousness, some mourner see stars of hope in the night of affliction, or some saint be quickened to let his light shine more brightly before men, that they by seeing his " good works may be led to glorify their Father which is in Heaven," the desire of the author will be realized.

J. W. THOMAS.

Providence, R. I., Feb. 6, 1875.

CONTENTS.

1*

THE MORNING STAR.

" I am the bright and morning star."

WHAT a great variety of figures are employed in the Scriptures to represent the Saviour!   He is called the Way, the Door, the Vine, the Rock, the Fountain, the Physician, the Shepherd, the Advo-cate, the Bridegroom, the Captain, the Forerunner, the Branch, the Prince of Life, the Sun of Righteousness, and many other names and titles, all of which show forth his fulness, the excellency of his character, and furnish subjects for useful meditation.   In the little text which I have chosen as the starting point of this discourse, he is represented as the Bright and Morning Star.   It is the name by which he called himself among the con cluding utterances of that sublime reve-lation which was given to John on the

Isle of Patmos. "I, Jesus, have sent mine angel to testify unto you these things in the churches. I am the root and the offspring of David, and the bright and morning star."—Rev. 22 : 16.

It is remarkable that in the opening and closing periods of the Christian dispensation, he is represented by a star. There is something very beautiful and expressive in this figure. A star.

Who that admires beauty, does not like to stand on a hill-top, or sail on the water, or sit in some door-yard, on a mild summer evening, and gaze up into the starry heavens? After the sun has gone down behind the western hills, one by one the little stars come peeping out, until all heaven is ablaze with their glory.

> " I gaze on heaven's etherial dome,
>   Star-spangled canopy of night,
>   And in imagination roam
>   Amid those radiant orbs of light."

The stars were made to *shine*. . They spread their beauty through the heavens, and make earth and sea radiant with celestial brightness. Night would be almost unendurable were there no stars to illuminate its darkness, but the Lord has wisely placed these lights in the fir-mament of heaven to cheer the sailor on the deep, the traveller in the wilderness, and to make glad the pathway of his children in this world. "And the Lord said, Let there be lights in the firma-ment of heaven : let them be for signs and for seasons, and to give light upon the earth."—GEN. 1 . 15. The stars not only give light, but they display their Creator's wisdom and glory. "The heav-ens declare the glory of God, and the firmament showeth his handiwork."

For the same reasons is the Saviour called a star. He is given for "signs" and for "seasons," to shed "light upon the earth," and to "declare the glory of God."

Was there ever such a bright luminary in the history of mankind ? There have indeed been other stars, and bright ones too, but none ever shone with such brightness as the morning star.

There was Enoch and Noah, who lived in the days before the flood; Abraham, Isaac, Jacob, Joseph, Moses, Joshua, Elijah, Samuel, David, Isaiah, and many others, who shone brightly in their time, but the brilliancy of Immanuel surpassed them all. The rising of this Star had long been foretold. One of old exclaimed when the spirit of prophecy came upon him, "There shall come a star out of Jacob; and a sceptre shall rise out of Israel." Num. xxiv. 17. And another prophesied. "The Lord himself shall give you a sign; behold a virgin shall conceive, and bear a son, and shall call his name Immanuel." Isa. vii. 14. When at length the time had arrived for these predictions to be fulfilled, a star appears in the eastern sky, and "wise men," laden with costly presents, start out in search of a new born sovereign. Coming to Jerusalem, they inquire, saying, "Where is he that is born King of the Jews? for we have seen his star in the east, and are come to worship him." Having received instruction where he was to be born, and leaving "king Herod and all the city troubled," they set out for Bethlehem, and "lo, the star which they saw in the east," leads the procession, and goes before them until it stands over where the young child was. It halts not at the palace of royalty or the home of wealth, where the young prince may recline on beds of down, but guides them to a stable, where they find a brighter " Star," robed in " swaddling clothes," and cradled in a manger. Here with a stable for his palace and a manger for his throne, they pay their first act of worship to him who is destined, ere long, to outrival in his shining all the monarchs of the universe. Angels announced his birth to the shepherds and made the night air resound with celestial music, singing " Glory to God in the highest, on earth peace and good will toward men." Surely a Bright

Star has appeared. He can be none other than the Son of God, " the brightness of his Father's glory and the express image of His person."

1. He shines with the brightness of *Purity.* What innocence and purity shone around him while an infant in his mother's arms. He was called a " holy child." Though partaking of human nature, born in a sinful world, surrounded by sinful influences, and associating with sinful beings, yet he was without sin. No dark spot of evil was ever found upon him. He was tempted in all points like as others, but he did not yield to temptation. He passed through the world without soiling his garments. Purity dwelt in his thoughts, dropped from his lips and flashed in his eye. He did no sin, neither was guile found in his mouth. Wherever he went purity sparkled and danced around his pathway, like dewdrops in the morning starlight.

2. He shines with the brightness of

Wisdom. He possessed a brilliant intellect. There was nothing dull or clumsy about his imagination. His perception was quick and clear. His thoughts were sharp and pointed. He was always ready with an answer to any question which might be asked him. At the age of twelve years, he was found in the temple with the doctors and lawyers, asking and answering questions that astonished them. During his ministry his teachings were simple and plain. His parables and illustrations were drawn from every day life. The children could understand him, and the common people heard him gladly, yet there was such a depth of wisdom in his utterances, that he took the wise in their own craftiness and discomfited all his foes. On one occasion when certain individuals had been sent to take him, they returned and said, "Never man spake like this man." He drew waters from the eternal depths, and unfolded truths such as men never heard before. In him were hid

all the treasures of wisdom and knowledge.   The wisdom of Solomon was
great, but a greater than Solomon was
here.

3.   He shines with the brightness of
Grace.   Here his brightness exceeds all
power of human conception.   No hu·
man intellect can fully comprehend the
wonders of redeeming grace.   Yet much
of its splendor is seen.   It was grace
that brought him into this world.

The law was given by Moses, but
grace and truth came by Jesus Christ.
He unfolded to men the character of his
Father.   God so loved the world, that
he gave his only begotten Son, that whosoever believeth in him, should not perish, but have everlasting life.   Ye know
the grace of our Lord Jesus Christ, that,
though he was rich, yet for your sakes
he became poor, that ye through his
poverty might be rich.   2 Cor. viii.: 9.
What condescension was this?   Had the
brightest archangel been commissioned
to come down from heaven with the

olive branch of peace in his hand, signi-
fying his Eternal Maker's readiness to
be reconciled; on our bended knees,
with tears of joy, and a torrent of thank-
fulnes , we ought to have received the
transporting news; but when instead of
such an angelic envoy, he sends his only
begotten Son, his Son beyond all thought
illustrious, to make us the gracious over-
ture; sends him from the habitations of
his holiness and glory, to put on the infirmities of mortality, and dwell among
sinful men; sends him not barely to
make us a transient visit, but to abide
many years in our inferior and miserable world; sends him not to exercise
dominion over monarchs, but to wear
out his life in the ignoble form of a *servant;* and, at last, to make his exit under the infamous character of a malefactor! Was there ever love like this? Did
ever grace stoop so low? Should the
sun be shorn of all his radiant honors,
and degraded into a *clod* of the valleys;
should all the dignitaries of heaven be

deposed from their thrones, and degene·
rate into insects of a day, great, great
would be the abasement; but *nothing*
to thine, most blessed Jesus ; nothing to
thine, thou Prince of Peace ; when, for
us men and for our salvation, thou did'st
not abhor the coarse accommodations of
the *manger :* thou did'st not decline the
gloomy horrors of the *grave.* He died
yet he lives.   For

4.   He shines with the brightness of
Immortality.   He was not a meteor or a
shooting star flashing through the dark·
ness with a sudde i brightness and then
disappearing, leaving the darkness more
intense than before.   No ! He shines
with a steady perpetual brilliancy.   He
is the same yesterday, to-day and for·
ever.

Other lights have shone brightly for
a time and then disappeared.   All the
great and good of past ages have passed
away.   They blessed the world while
they lived, but their light was soon ob·
scured in the darkness of death.   Not

so with this star. He ever liveth. In the days of his flesh men tried to prevent him from shining. They persecuted him, lied about him, threw the mud and dirt of slander at him, but still he shone. They denied him, falsely accused him, spit in his face, stripped him of his raiment, clothed him in purple, crowned him with thorns, crucified him, buried him, and guarded his sepulchre.

But on the morning of the third day he shone with greater splendor than ever. His sufferings and death were only dark clouds that passed before him, leaving him to shine on with the brightness of an "endless life." He broke the fetters of death, and ascended on high amid clouds of glory and hosts of shining angels. Stephen, in his dying hour, and Paul on his way to Damascus, caught glimpses of his glory as he shone down from above, and John on the Isle of Patmos, saw him in unparalleled brightness, and heard his voice saying "I am he that liveth and was dead; and behold, I am alive, for evermore, and have the keys of death and the grave. Rev. i. 18.   But Jesus is not only a "bright star;" he is also the "morning star."   He has *pre-eminence* above all other stars.   He shines not toward sun-setting but toward sunrising.   He is not the harbinger of night but of morn. Shining as the day begins to break, he gives token of *advancing light.*   Was it not a *day dawn* when he first shone forth from Bethlehem ?   The world was sleeping in the darkness of sin and ig-norance.   Rome, Greece, Egypt and Babylon, with all their learning, knew not the true God.   The Jewish Church was in a formal backslidden condition. Holy prophets, who saw the rising of that star in vision had passed away. Only now and then were a few holy watchers, who waited for the consola-tion of Israel.   Good old Simeon being led by the Spirit into the temple, when the young child was brought in, took the infant Savior in his arms, and blessed

God, and said, " Lord now lettest thou thy servant depart in peace, according to thy word, for mine eyes have seen thy salvation which thou hast prepared before the face of all people. A light to lighten the Gentiles and the glory of thy people Israel. Luke, ii. 28–29. Anna also, the prophetess, who departed not from the temple, but served God day and night with fastings and prayers, " coming in that same instant gave thanks likewise unto the Lord, and spake of him to all them that looked for redemption in Jerusalem." Was not this star beautiful and glorious to those faithful ones, who had watched so long for the morning light? A better day was near at hand. Zacharias also whose tongue was loosed after the birth of John, caught sight of the approaching day beams, and exclaimed, " thou, child, shalt be called the prophet of the Highest, for thou shalt go before the face of the Lord to prepare his ways; to give knowledge of salvation unto his people by the remission of their sins, through the tender mercy of our God; whereby the day spring from on high hath visited us, to give light to them that sit in darkess and in the shadow of death, to guide our feet into the way of peace." Luke i. 76–79. A few years pass and the voice of a strange looking man is heard crying in the wilderness of Judea, "Prepare ye the way of the Lord make his paths straight." The whole region is stirred. Light is breaking. A great reformation sweeps through the commu·nity. "Then went out to him Jerusalem, and all Judea, and all the region round about Jordan, and were baptized of him in Jordan, confessing their sins." The proud, self-righteous Pharisees and Sadducees, hear of this strange preacher's wonderful success, and they go out to see what he is doing. When John saw them, he lifted up his strong, heart-searching voice and said, "O, generation of vipers, who hath warned you to flee from the wrath to come? Bring forth therefore fruits meet for repentance : or answerable to amendment of life. And think not to say within yourselves, We have Abraham to our Father : for I say unto you, that God is able of these stones to raise up children unto Abraham. And now also the axe is laid unto the root of the trees ; therefore every tree which bringeth not forth good fruit is hewn down and cast into the fire. I indeed baptize you with water unto repentance : but he that cometh after me is mightier than I, whose shoes I am not worthy to bear : he shall baptize you with the Holy Ghost, and with fire : Whose fan is in his hand, and he will thoroughly purge his floor, and gather his wheat into the garner; but he will burn up the chaff with unquenchable fire. Then cometh Jesus from Galilee to Jordan unto John to be baptized of him. But John forbade him, saying, I have need to be baptized of thee, and comest thou to me ? And Jesus answering said unto him, suffer it

to be so now: for thus it becometh us to
fulfil all righteousness. Then he suffered
him.   And Jesus when he was baptized;
came up straightway out of the water,
and, lo, the heavens were opened unto
him, and he saw the Spirit of God, de-
scending like a dove, and lighting upon
him: And lo, a voice from heaven, saying, This is my beloved Son, in whom
I am well pleased. Matt. iii. 3.   John
the Baptist soon disappears. "He was
a burning and a shining light," but he
had fulfilled his mission, and pointing
his disciples to the One who was greater
than himself said, "Behold the Lamb
of God which taketh away the sin of
the world."

The bright and Morning Star now
begins to ascend, rising higher and shining brighter, until his fame is spread far
and wide.   Coming from the wilderness
where he had been "tempted of the
devil," he begins preaching, and performing miracles with wonderful power.
Passing through the villages and towns,

" he came to Nazareth, where he had been brought up; and as his custom was, he went into the synagogue on the sabbath day, and stood up for to read. And there was delivered unto him the book of the prophet Isaiah. And when he had opened the book, he found the place where it was written, " The spirit of the Lord is upon me, because he hath anointed me to preach the gospel to the poor ; he hath sent me to heal the broken hearted, to preach deliverance to the captives, and recovering of sight to the blind, to set at liberty them that are bruised, to preach the acceptable year of the Lord." And the eyes of all them that were in the synagogue were fastened on him. And he began to say unto them " This day is this scripture fulfilled in your ears. And all bear him witness and wondered at the gracious words which proceeded out of his mouth. Luke iv. 16, 17. Is it any wonder that they listened attentively to such a preacher ? The words he spake were "gracious words,"—-words full of grace. A new era had dawned. The long looked for Messiah had appeared. How highly favored were this people who listened to his voice, and saw the " shining of his power."

Many prophets and righteous men had desired to see this day, but had not seen it: It was the day of grace, the day of salvation. Multitudes flocked to hear the wonderful preacher. By the seaside, in the wilderness, and on the mountain top, he proclaimed the words of everlasting life. Is it not astonishing that he should be rejected by the Jews; Yet so it was. He came to his own, and his own received him not, but as many as did receive him, to them gave he power to become the sons of God. His followers were mostly from among the poor. Not in Jerusalem among the doctors and lawyers did he find men to be his apostles, but to the fishermen of Galilee he said, "Follow me, and I will make you fishers of men."

They followed him, and with these he traveled, and toiled, and suffered. With these he watched, and wept, and prayed, with these he established his covenant, and left his parting benediction. To these he gave the last great commission, "Go ye into all the world, and preach the gospel to every creature." Christ's ministery was short. Only a few years did the world have the benefit of his personal ministrations. While he was "in the world" he was the "light of the world" but when he went away he left his church to carry forward the great work of spreading the gospel, and to be witnesses of his resurrection. The church was now to be the light of the world. From the day of Pentecost where they were all filled with the Holy Ghost the light went forth. Every believer was a bright star. With wonderful ra-pidity the truth spread. Everywhere men heard the story of Bethlehem and of Calvary. Notwithstanding opposition and persecution raged, yet with wonder-

ful " power gave the apostles witness of ·
his resurrection." They affirmed that the
Christ who had been crucified, and
buried, was alive again, and had ascended on high. The word of God grew
mightily and prevailed. The old dispensation had passed away, and the day
of gospel grace had been ushered
in. The Morning Star was beginning to
shed his beams over the dark nations of
the earth. Since then the world has
been lightened with his gospel. Un-
numbered sinners in every land have
caught sight of his glorious beams, and
rejoiced in his heavenly light. Over
eighteen centuries have passed away and
still angels around the throne wait to
rejoice over repenting sinners. This
work, however, will not always continue
Another change is coming. If the *first* rising of this Star ushered in the morning of
Grace, His *second* rising will usher in the
morning of *Glory.* A better day yet
awaits this world—a day when all darkness shall take its flight, a day when there

shall be no more sin, when iniquity
shall come to an end, when "evil work·
ers," and those who love "darkness better than light" shall be destroyed, when
crime shall be done away, when there
shall be no more wars, strife, or divis·
ions in church or state, when there shall
be no more poverty, no more financial
failures, no more oppression, no more
groans, and sorrows, and heartaches, no
more watching by sick beds, no more
farewells to the dying, no more weep·
ings for the dead, but a day when there
shall be peace, and light, and love, and
joy unutterable, when loved ones shall
meet and righteousness prevail, and
death be destroyed, and the curse be re·
moved, and the "glory of God fill the
earth, as the waters do the sea." That
day will have its morning. Christ is the
Morning Star. "I am the root and offspring of David, and the bright and
morning-star." "And this name is given
to him not only because of the glory of
his person and the brightness of his ap·

pearing, but because of the *time* when
he is to appear.

The first act at his appearing, when
he comes in glory—the first indication
of his arrival, while yet aloft " in the
air," is likened to the shining of the
Morning-star. Afterwards he shall come
forth as " the Sun of righteousness," fill-
ing the whole earth with his brightness,
and shadowing the nations with his
healing wings, (Mal. iv: 2.) ; but at
first he shows himself as the Morning-
star—big with the hope of day, yet not
the day, brighter than all other stars
and eclipsing all of them, yet not the
Day-star ; forerunner of the sun, yet not
the sun ; foreteller of the dawn, yet not
the dawn.

" Fairest of stars, last in the train of night,
If better thou belong not to the dawn:
Sure pledge of day, that crown'st the smiling morn
With thy bright circlet, praise him in thy sphere,
While day arises, that sweet hour of prime."

We read in scripture of the eyelids
of the morning ; and the morning star is

the first beam shooting from under these lids as they begin to re-open, that the eye of day may again irradiate the earth. It is only they who awake early that see the first opening of these eyelids, or gaze upon the morning-star, or breathe the morning freshness, or taste the morning dew. So is it with those of whom it is said, " Blessed and holy is he that hath part in, the first resurrection." To them come the quickening words, "Awake and sing, ye that dwell in dust." Isa. xxvi. 19. Into their tomb the earliest ray of glory finds its way. They drink in the first gleams of morning, while as yet the eastern clouds give but the faintest signs of its uprising. Its genial fragrance, its soothing stillness, its bracing freshness, its sweet loveliness, its quiet purity, all so solemn and yet so full of hope, these are theirs. Oh the contrast between these things and the dark night through which they have passed! Oh the contrast between these things and the

3*

grave from which they have sprung! And as they shake off the encumber-ing turf, flinging mortality aside, and rising, in glorified bodies, to meet their Lord in the air, they are lighted and guided upward, along the untrod-den pathway, by the beams of that Star of morning, which, like the Star of Bethlehem, conducts them to the presence of the King. There seems to be more *periods* than one (if times so very brief may be called by that name) opening out upon us when the Lord comes. Just as there are more *scenes* than one, and more *acts* than one, in the "day of the Lord," so there are more periods than one. And it is interesting to notice these in connection with the Morn-ing Star.

All the time up to the moment of his appearing is reckoned *night*. Then the scenes change, and, step by step, the day with its full sunshine is brought in. First, there is *the period of the Morning-Star*, during which the dead saints awake and the living saints are changed; then that which is sown in corruption is raised in incorruption, that which is sown in dishonor is raised in glory, that which is sown in weakness is raised in power, that which is sown a natural body is raised a spiritual body; and then they that have long dwelt in dust awake and sing. In every land they have found a grave, and every land now gives up the sleeping clay. They come forth "in the beauties of holiness from the womb of the morning," like the ten thousand times ten thousand dew-drops of the night, made visible by the morning-star, and sparkling to its far coming glory. (Ps. cx. 3; Isa. xxvi. 19.) Next there is *the period of the Twilight.*

This is the time when " the light shall not be clear nor dark," like " the morning spread upon the mountains." (Joel ii. 2.) Then has the last battle strife begun; then the Lord with his rod of iron is breaking his enemies in pieces like a potter's vessel; then he cometh forth from his place to punish the in-habitants of the earth for their iniquity; then, with all his saints, he executes the infinite vengeance, destroys Anti-Christ, lays waste the world with sore calamity and purging fire.

Next there is *The Morning*. The enemy has disappeared; each wreck that marked his dominion or his destruction is gone. The face of the earth is re-newed, the storm is laid to rest, and the glory of an unclouded sun and an un-sullied firmament makes creation sing for joy. The voice of the Beloved is heard, " Rise up, my love, my fair one, and come away. For lo, the winter is past, the rain is over and gone; the flow-ers appear on the earth; the time of the singing of birds is come, and the voice of the turtle is heard in our land; the fig tree putteth forth her green figs, and the vines with the tender grape give a good smell. Arise, my love, my fair one, and come away." (Sol. Song. ii. 10-13.)

Lastly, there is *The Day* in its full brightness. For the path of this Just One is like the shining light that shineth more and more unto the perfect day. Of that day earth has never seen the like. For that day it waits in patient hope, struggling hard, meanwhile, with darkness, and labouring to throw off its long sad weight of ill.

It is as if the glory of the Lord, when first coming in sight of the earth, showed itself in the far distance, as the star of morning; token most welcome and hopeful, recognized at once by those who knew the true light of the world, and who had often in other days looked out wistfully for the Star of Jacob. It is *next*, as if the same glory when it neared the earth, showed itself in terrible majesty as the sign of the Son of man, in seeing which all the tribes of the earth mourn; for just as *in the morning watch* the Lord looked through the pillar of fire and cloud and troubled the host of the Egyptians, so, when he cometh with clouds " all kindreds of the earth shall wail because of him." It is, *next*, as if the same glory of the Son of man, coming still nearer, took up its destined position, and spread its skirts over earth as did the pillar-cloud over the tents of Israel. It is, *lastly*, as if this glory, this more than shechinah splendor, showed itself as the Sun of righteousness, bearing healing in his wings, wherewith he heals the *nations*, so that the inhabitants shall no more say I am sick; wherewith he heals the *earth*, so that the curse takes its flight; wherewith he heals the *air*, so that it poisons no more. Then day shall utter speech to day in a way unheard of before; then shall their lines go throughout all the earth, and their words to the end of the world, when out of that " tabernacle which he hath set for the Sun," that Sun shall come forth as a bridegroom out of his chamber, rejoicing as a strong man to run a race. Then shall come to pass the saying that is written, " Behold the glory of the God of Israel came from the way of the east, and his voice was like the noise of many waters, *and the earth shined with his glory.*" Ezek. xliii. 2.

Then will he "destroy in this mountain the face of the covering cast over all people, and the vail that is spread over all nations. He will swallow up death in victory; and the Lord God will wipe away tears from off all faces; and the rebuke of his people shall he take away from off all the earth: for the Lord hath spoken it. And it shall be said in that day, Lo, this is our God; we have waited for him, and he will save us: this is the Lord; we have waited for him we will be glad and rejoice in his salva. tion. In that day shall this song be sung in the land of Judah. We have a strong city; salvation will God appoint for walls and bulwarks. Open ye the gates, that the righteous nation which keepeth the truth may enter in." Isa. xxv. 7, 8, 9, and xxvi. 1, 2. Then shall the "wilderness and the solitary place be glad for them; and the desert shall rejoice, and blossom as the rose. It shall blossom abundantly, and rejoice even with joy and singing: the glory of Lebanon shall be given unto it, the excellency of Carmel and Sharon, they shall see the glory of the Lord, and the excellency of our God." Isa. xxxv. 1, 2. Then shall "violence no more be heard in thy land, wasting nor destruction within thy borders; but thou shalt call thy walls Salvation, and thy gates Praise. The sun shall be no more thy light by day; neither for brightness shall the moon give light unto thee; for the Lord shall be thine everlasting light, and the days of thy mourning shall be ended. Thy people also shall be all righteous: they shall inherit the land forever." Isa. lx. 18, 19, 20. That day of glory, of resurrection, and eternal blessedness is hastening apace. Just how soon the Morning Star will appear I cannot say. The night is far spent, the day is at hand. Wise will we be if we are found with our "loins girded about, and our lights burning, and we like unto men that wait for their Lord. That when he cometh, and knocketh, we may open to him immediately." Blessed are those servants, whom the Lord when he cometh shall find watching. The true church will not be asleep. She will be awake, and anxiously looking out to behold the first glimmerings of morning light. "But ye, brethren, are not in darkness, that that day should overtake you as a thief. Ye are all the children of light, and the children of the day: we are not of the night, nor of darkness. Therefore let us not sleep, as do others; but let us watch and be sober. For they that sleep sleep in the night; and they that be drunken are drunken in the night. But let us, who are of the day, be sober, putting on the breastplate of faith and love; and for a helmet, the hope of sal·vation." 1 Thes. v. 4–8.

It was the "wise virgins" who took "oil in their vessels with their lamps,"

when they " went forth to meet the bride·
groom," and it is " unto them that *look
for him*" that he shall appear the " second time without sin unto salvation."
Signs in the moral, physical, religious
and political world proclaim the morning
near. " We have also a more sure word
of prophecy ; whereunto ye do well that
ye take heed, as unto a light that shin·
eth in a dark place, until the *day dawn*,
and the *day-star* arise." 2 Pet. i. 19.
As sailors on the deep, tossed by restless storms, look out for some guiding
star by which they may reach the de·
sired haven, so—

" We who long the wrath have borne,
  Of heaving surge and wailing wind,
Look out to hail the endless morn,
  And watch its harbingers to find.

Oh, that our Day-Star may arise,
  Resplendent o'er the gloom of night,
And bless the longing watchers' eyes,
  With promise of unfading light."

What *now* is the duty of every christian ? Is it not to *shine?* Not to shine

with worldly pomp or splendor, not with wealth or high sounding titles, but to shine with the brightness of " pure religion." The world is in darkness, it needs light. They who were " sometimes darkness, but who are now light in the Lord, should let their light so shine before men that others by seeing their good works might be led to glorify God." As the stars are *receptive* of light from the Sun, and can only shine as they are shone upon, so the christian must receive his light from Christ. He is the great light. From him we must receive the light of truth, of grace, and salvation. It is He that calls us out of darkness into his marvelous light. It is His spirit that illuminates our minds, and enables us to walk in the light, as He is in the light, and to have fellowship one with another. The entrance of His word giveth light. It is a light to our path, and a lamp to our feet. As the pillar of cloud and of fire went before the Israelites, lighting up their pathway through the wilderness, and guiding them toward the promised land, so Christ is the light of his people, following him they do not walk in darkness but have the light of life. If we follow on to know the Lord, we shall know his goings forth prepared as the morning, and we shall be able to say with the Psalmist, the Lord is my light and my salvation, whom shall I fear, the Lord is the strength of my life of whom shall I be afraid. Our path-way will grow brighter and brighter even unto the perfect day. Having then received light from Christ we are to let it shine. Be *reflectors*. Let your re-ligion shine out in every thought, word and act. Do not try to *make* your light shine, but *let* it shine. Religion is not something put on, it is a principle and a power in the heart, that controls the life and keeps it in harmony with the divine word. It is God working in us both to will and to do of his good pleasure. We are not to live for ourselves. If we are wise it will be our desire and aim to

"turn many to righteousness." There
are several ways by which we may do
this. First, we may do it by the charm
of a right *Example*. All our efforts will
amount to but little, unless we live right.
I have read a fable something like this.
A child, coming from a filthy home was
taught at school to wash its face. It
went home so much improved in appearance that its mother washed *her* face.
And when the father of the household
came home and saw the improvement in
domestic appearance, he washed *his* face.
The neighbors happening in, saw the
change and tried the same experiment,
until all that street was purified, and the
next street copied its example, and the
whole city felt the result of one school-
boy washing his face. The best way to
get the world washed of its sins and pol-
lutions is to have our own heart cleaned
and purified. Nothing can take the
place of personal religion. A man with
grace in his heart, cheerfulness in his
face, and holy consistency in his beha-

4*

vior, is a perpetual sermon. He shines wherever he goes. In the prayer meeting, in his .home, on the street, in the workshop, he is a living epistle read and known of all men. When Moses came down from the Mount where he had been communing with God, his face shone. So the man who lives his religion from day to day, will have a radiance about him that will attract the attention of others. Men will take knowledge of him that he has been with Jesus. Let your light shine then by setting a right example.

We may turn many to righteousness by *Prayer*. An earnest christian worker once told me that "he knew of *fifty* persons who had been converted to God in answer to his prayers." Is not this encouraging? Prayer will often accomplish what nothing else will. There is no such detective as prayer, for no one can hide away from it. It puts its hand on the shoulder of a man five thousand miles off. The boy who runs away from home and goes to sea, may get beyond the sound of his mother's voice but he cannot get beyond the reach of her prayers. An answer to prayer may touch a ship in mid ocean. Through prayer we may send telegraphic dispatches all over the world. Along the coast there are fog bells erected which are rung in foggy weather to warn mariners of danger. We can alarm men by prayer when they are lost in the fog and darkness of sin. Prayer has done wonders. By the breath of prayer Elijah blew the clouds all out of heaven, and there was no rain for three years and six months. By the breath of prayer he blew them back again and there was an abundance of rain. By prayer Samuel brought thunder and lightning from heaven. By prayer Joshua caught the Sun by its golden bit and it stood still. By prayer Daniel tamed the lions in their den. By prayer the three worthies walked unharmed through the fiery furnace. By prayer the Holy Spirit came down on the day of pentecost and three thousand souls were converted. By prayer Paul and Silas tore open the prison doors and shattered the foundations of the Philippian jail. There is no weapon so mighty as prayer. No person was ever yet converted without it. If we are christians it is because somebody prayed for us. No person can be saved without prayer. By prayer *all* can work. If you cannot preach you can pray. If you cannot write you can pray. If you cannot sing you can pray. A minister once called on a member of his church who was confined to a sick bed. He found her mourning to think that she was of so little benefit to any one. Said he, " You are one of the most useful members of my church, for when I am preaching I know that you are praying for me." Pray on, pray on ye afflicted saints. Your prayers may bring many sinners to repentance. Praying breath was never spent in vain. If you wish to shine in this world as a living Christian, then pray much. Pray short, pray earnest, pray often, pray always. Without ceasing, make mention of some one in prayer every day. Again, we may turn many to righteousness by *Personal effort.* If we would find the lost sheep we must *go after it.* Speak to somebody. Do not wait until you can make a formal speech. One word may be all that is needed. What multitudes there are who go to church from week to week, and yet who never speak to a sinner, nor make any personal effort to lead souls to Christ. I heard of a minister who preached from this subject. " Recognition of friends in the future world." A gentleman was heard to remark on going out, " I think the minister would do well to preach about recognition of friends in *this* world, for I have attended this church *twenty years, and not one of the members has ever spoken to me.*" There is too much of this preaching at arms length. We must *come down* and *talk with* the people if we would do them good. A kind word, a smile, a shake of the hand, a little tract given, has often been the means of turning men from the error of their ways. Much good may be accomplished by going from house to house, talking and praying with families, inviting them to meeting, and making them feel that you have an interest for them. Jesus went about doing good. He came to seek and to save the lost. Wherever he found a poor, bruised, penitent heart, he poured in the oil of consolation. No christian should be idle. Each and every one has a work to perform. We need not go far away. There is plenty to do near our own house. Begin right where you are. When Andrew had found the Savior, he went and called his brother Simon and saith unto him, " We have found the Messias, and he brought him to Jesus." Go and do the same Be not contented to bring *one*, bring *many*. What an inducement we have to labor for the salvation of souls. Daniel says, " They that be wise shall shine as the brightness of the firmament, and they that turn many to righteousness, as he stars for. ever and ever." What a reward will this be! As we look up into the sky, we notice that each star shines with a *Distinct*, a *separate* glory. So it will be with the saints. In that future world we shall not lose our individuality. Each one will have his own body, occupy his own place, wear his own crown, shine with his own glory. In this world some of the best christians are overlooked, un. noticed, unappreciated. They are crowded out, pushed one side, trodden down, and sometimes lost sight of amid the bustle and confusion of earth. Not so there. Heaven is large enough to give all a place. There will be a mani. festation ot the sons of God. Christ will call for his "hidden ones." Not one shall there be overlooked. Putting around them the mantle of his glory, they shall shine separately, distinctly, " as the stars for ever and ever."

Notice again, that the stars shine in

Groups. In looking up, you find the worlds in family circles. Orion in a group. The Pleiades in a group. The solar system is like a family of children with bright faces, gathered around one great fireplace. The planets do not wander off, and lose sight of each other. They go in squadrons and fleets, sailing through immensity. There will be family groups in Heaven. The saints shall dwell in neighborhoods and clusters. Yonder I see a constellation of Patri-archs. Noah with some of his family who were saved in the ark. Abraham with his children, who were sojourners in a strange land. Jacob with his sons. Moses with some whom he led through the wilderness. Yonder by the river of life, I see a group of prophets and apos-tles. How brightly they shine, how peacefully they dwell together. Yon-der, under the tree of life I see a clus-ter of martyrs, who came out of great tribulation, and washed their robes and made them white in the blood of the

Lamb. Yonder is Latimer and Ridley, and John Huss, who were faithful unto death. Yonder is John Bunyan who has now reached the Celestial City he so beautifully described. O yes, all around amid the groves, and on the hillsides of Paradise I see family circles. There we shall visit each other, talk together, and never be afraid of sickness or separation. Is this so? "They shall come from the east, from the west, from the north and from the south, and shall sit down in the kingdom of God." Luke xiii. 29. Yes, we shall shine in family groups, "as the stars forever and ever."

Again, they shall shine as the stars in *Number.* Who can count the stars? In a clear night we can see countless multitudes of shining orbs. It was said to one of old, "Thy seed shall be as the stars of heaven, and as the sand on the sea shore, innumerable." There are some who think only *their* sect will shine in glory. They only have the truth, they are the chosen ones, and none can be saved except they follow them, and subscribe to their creed. Elijah once got this sectarian spirit. He said, "Lord, they have digged down thine altars, slain thy prophets, and I only am left." But the Lord answered him, "I have yet seven thousand men who have not bowed the knee to Baal." The Lord still has his people. We are mistaken, if in our narrow mindedness we shut out all who do not believe as we do, or who do not belong to our church. All over the land, in cities and towns, in nooks and corners, on mountains and in valleys, are those who have the mark of the good Shepherd. How many did John see when he had a vision of the redeemed? First he says, " I saw an hundred and forty and four thousand which were sealed out of the twelve tribes of the children of Israel." What else did you see, John? " After this I beheld, and lo, a great multitude, which no man could number, of all nations and kindreds, and people, and tongues, stood before the throne and before the Lamb, clothed with white robes and palms in their hands. Rev. vii. 9.

O yes, there will be a countless multitude in that better world. In numbers they will shine " as the stars forever and ever."

Again, the stars of heaven shine in *Harmony.* The planets move with great speed, yet there is no collision, no grating, no running across each others track. All the worlds of light that whirl through space are in harmony. There will be no discord among the redeemed. In this world there is much that is out of order. The machinery of nations grates and chafes fearfully. In the church there are strifes and divisions. All do not see things alike. Creation groans and travails in pain awaiting a better day. Here there is no complete and abiding harmony. There is antagonism, opposition in all circles. In the world to come there will be none of this. All the wrongs of earth will then be rectified. Everything will be harmonious. No discord in the music of heaven. "And they sung a new song, saying, Thou art worthy to take the book, and to open the seals thereof: for thou wast slain, and hast redeemed us to God by thy blood out of every nation; and hast made us unto our God kings and priests: and we shall reign on the earth." Rev. v, 9. In sweet and undisturbed harmony will they shine "as the stars forever and ever."

Again, they shall shine as the stars in *Perpetuity.* The same stars that look down upon us looked down on the shepherds of Bethlehem. The stars that fought against Sisera, in their their courses, wear the same bright armor to-night. When Adam and Eve walked in the garden of Eden in the cool of the day, they saw the same stars which we behold. To the ancients the stars were symbols of eternity. The saints shall live forever. All things here fade and pass away. The grass withers, the flowers die, the leaves fade. Change and decay is indelibly written upon every object around us. Man partakes of the general instability. He is mortal. He comes forth like a flower, and continueth not. The earth itself shall pass away. But it will not be so in the heavenly world. The kingdom promised is an everlasting kingdom. The bodies of the redeemed will be immortal bodies. This mortal shall put on immortality, this corruptible incorruption. The crowns they wear will be fadeless crowns. The life they live will be eternal life. The song they sing will be an endless song. The glory they enter into will be perpetual glory. The brightness with which they shine will be an everlasting brightness, " for they that be wise shall shine as the brightness of the firmament, and they that turn many to righteousness as the stars for ever and ever."

ON THE LOOKOUT.

MARK XIII. 37.

" What I say unto you, I say unto all, Watch."

" Live and learn" is a motto which every individual capable of learning should adopt. We are never too old to learn. We should begin when we are young and keep on learning all the way through life. Learn from everybody, from everything and in every place. Wherever we go we should keep our eyes open, and never think ourselves too wise to learn more, or too good to improve. " Mind not high things but condescend to men of low estate. Be not wise in your own conceits," are injunctions which we shall do well to always bear in mind. Seldom do I take a walk in the field, ride along the road, journey in the cars, or sail on the water, but what I see something to instruct, and to suggest thoughts for my practical improvement. Not long ago I had occasion to take a journey of nearly two hundred miles in the night season. Thinking it might be pleasanter to go by water, I stepped on board of a noble steamer, and was soon gliding sweetly away over the billows. It was a beautiful moonlight evening, and as the captain was a friend of mine I spent much of the time in the pilot-house, talking and gazing at whatever might be seen along the coast. Not long after having left the wharf, I noticed that one man took his position on the bow of the boat, and kept constantly walking around on the deck, and looking out on either side and ahead, to see what might be seen. At first I supposed he would only remain there until the vessel got out of the harbor; but seeing that he continued in this position far into the hours of night, I inquired what it meant, as I was not fully acquainted with the manner of running steamboats, and I

really began to have some sympathy
for the man who was taking so much
of the cold sea breeze. "Oh," said the
captain, "he is the bow watch. He
watches there all night." As soon as
the steamer leaves the wharf, he takes
his position on the bow of the boat, and
watches through the night until morning. Whether the weather is cold or
warm, pleasant or unpleasant, still he
keeps at his post. He is employed for
this very purpose, and the law requires
every steamer to have a watchman.
Faithfully did he perform his duty. All
night long, as the vessel ploughed
through the waves, and while the passengers were quietly sleeping, he walked the deck, looked out for dangers, and
was ready to give the alarm in case he
saw anything that required it. How
suggestive was this circumstance to my
mind. When I came down from the
pilot-house, I could not pass him without quoting this passage of scripture,
"What I say unto you I say unto all,

watch." I thought here is a lesson for me. The Christian is a voyager. He is sailing along the coast of Time. It is night. Dangers and perils abound. There is no time to sleep. He must be on the lookout continually. Ministers of the gospel are set as watchmen on the walls of Zion. Their own safety and the safety of others depends upon their vigilance. If the watchman on the steamer had fallen asleep, who knows but that he and all the passengers would have found a watery grave? No doubt many to-day are sleeping in old ocean's depths the victims of some officer's unfaithfulness. And who knows how many men and women have gone down to the grave without hope in Christ, because the watchmen in Zion did not do their duty?

The Captain of our salvation has commanded us all to watch. We must watch ourselves that we keep alive and wide awake. We must watch our thoughts, words, and actions, that we do not fall into a stupid, drowsy, dreamy state of mind, or allow ourselves to become intoxicated with worldly pleasures and thereby be unfitted to discharge the spiritual duties of life. Watch unto prayer and be sober. We must remember our responsibility. Watch for souls. Perhaps some poor shipwrecked brother is struggling for life in the dark waters of sin and temptation. Give him your hand. Help him out. Throw the rope of salvation. Fling out the life-buoy. Tell him of Jesus, and of the blood that saves There are men and women all around us who need help. Let us watch for opportunities to speak to them some word of kindness. One word, one look, one tract given, may save a soul from death and place another star in your crown that shall sparkle forever and ever. Watch for dangers. Alarm the careless. Wake up the sleepers. Tell them there is danger ahead. The ship of Time will soon collide with the Judgment Throne.

See the breakers roll high on the lee shore of eternal destruction! Put on the life preservers. Flee from the wrath to come. Look aloft to Him who is able to save. Set your affections on things above, and then the attractions of heaven will be stronger than the attractions of earth, and when the Good Pilot appears, he will conduct you safely into the Celestial Harbor, and so you will be " forever with the Lord."

" What I say unto you, I say unto all. Watch !"

ABIDE IN THE SHIP.

"Except these abide in the ship, ye cannot be saved."

Paul was an old sailor; not from oc·cupation, but from frequency of travel. He knew what it was to be in "perils on the deep," and no doubt he could have taken a vessel across the Mediter·ranean quite as safely as any experi·enced sea captain. He was now making a trip to Rome, and this voyage, though one of the most perilous, was yet the most successful voyage he ever made. The ship was lost, but he had a blessed revival, and saved all on board, two hundred and seventy five souls. Paul was shipped as a prisoner, but he was promoted to captain, for he had the whole crew looking to him for salva·tion. It takes the Almighty to work wonders. He can send out a storm on the sea, and bring wicked sailors and soldiers to bow at his feet in answer to the prayers of a righteous prisoner. Had the centurion and managers of the ship heeded the advice given by Paul, much of the damage might have been avoided. He foresaw the danger to which they would be exposed and said to them, "Sirs, I perceive that this voyage will be with hurt and much damage; not only of the lading and ship, but also of our lives." So now, the Lord's servants often give good advice to the young, but it is not heeded, and consequently many are overtaken by the storms of sin and temptation. "Nevertheless, the centurion believed the master and the owner of the ship, more than those things which were spoken by Paul. And because the haven was not commodious to winter in, the more part advised to depart thence also, if by any means they might attain to Phenice, and there to winter; which is an haven

6

of Crete, and lieth toward the south-
west and northwest. And when the
south wind blew softly, supposing that
they had obtained their purpose, loosing
thence, they sailed close by Crete.

But not long after there arose against
it a tempestuous wind, called Eurocly-
don. And when the ship was caught,
and could not bear up into the wind,
we let her drive. And running under a
certain island which is called Clauda,
we had much work to come by the boat,
which when they had taken up, they
used helps, undergirding the ship; and,
fearing lest they should fall into the
quicksands, strake sail, and so were
driven. And we being exceedingly
tossed with a tempest, the next day they
lightened the ship. And the third day
we cast out with our own hands the
tackling of the ship. And when neither
sun nor stars in many days appeared,
and no small tempest lay on us, all hope
that we should be saved was then taken
away." What a scene to contemplate.

Two hundred and seventy-five souls in despair. The winds howled, the sea roared, the vessel tossed, no stars appeared—-"all hope that they should be saved was taken away." So it is in life, we like to have our own way, until God sends out some storm of affliction, and shows us that earthly hopes are vain, and that he alone can deliver. Man's extremity is God's opportunity. But were all on that vessel in despair? No. There was one who was calm and trustful. It was Paul. Far beyond the storm and clouds he could see the "bright and morning star." His faith did not waver. After long abstinence he stood forth in the midst of them and said. "Sirs, ye should have hearkened unto me, and not have loosed from Crete, and so have gained this harm and loss. And now I exhort you to be of good cheer; for there shall be no loss of any man's life among you, but of the ship. For there stood by me this night the angel of God, whose I am, and whom

I serve, saying, "Fear not, Paul, thou must be brought before Cæsar; and, lo, God hath given thee all them that sail with thee, Wherefore, sirs, be of good cheer; for I believe God that it shall be even as it was told me." Blessed faith that could triumph in the midst of uch a storm! What a strong refuge they have who trust in the living God. He is the God of the sea as well as of the land. Paul was now master of the whole company. God had exalted him in their midst, and they were now to obey his orders. " When the fourteenth night was come, and we were driven up and down in Adria, about midnight, the shipmen deemed that they drew near to some country. And sounded and found it twenty fathoms; and when they had gone a little further, they sounded again and found it fifteen fathoms. Then fearing lest we should have fallen upon rocks, they cast four anchors out upon the stern, and wished for the day. And as the shipmen were about to flee out of the ship, when they had let down the boat into the sea, Paul said to the centurion and to the soldiers, "Except these abide in the ship ye cannot be saved." Salvation depended on their abiding in the ship. Reader, are you in the gospel ship? Have you fled to Christ for salvation? Are you sailing toward the heavenly port? Abide in the ship. If storms arise and your sky is mantled with clouds look aloft. There is one who controls the winds and waves. Hear His voice louder than the tempest's roar." "Be of good cheer." Do not backslide. Stay on board. The storm will soon be over. The land heaves in view. The morning dawns. Wait. The captain will bring you safe into harbor.

> "Christ is my pilot wise,
>   My compass is his word;
>   My soul each storm defies,
>   Whilst I have such a lord,
>   I'll trust his faithfulness and power
>   To save me in the trying hour."

6*

THE DOUBTER'S VOYAGE.

Acts xxvii. 20.

" All hope that we should be saved, was then taken
away."

" My little barque is tempest tossed,
   Far out upon the billowy tide,
Alas! I fear it must be lost,
   It cannot long in safety ride ;
Above, below me, and around,
   Is murky darkuess, sea and cloud
Enfold me in the gloom profound,
   'Tis very like the dead man's shroud.

Auon I rise on billows high,
   Anou, sink down in caverns deep;
The sea-birds close about me fly,
   They scream, as o'er my head they sweep;
I see no giimmering beacon light,
   That sends its friendly rays to me,
To mark a path of silvery light,
   Through the black stygian turbid sea;

And gloomy doubts of unbelief,
   Have drifted me away so far
From all that can afford relief,
   And hide, by clouds, hope's beaming star,—

For *other* voyagers there *may be*,
  A beacon and a haven fair,
Alas ! alas ! there is none for me,
  I shall go down in dark despair.

I would be saved, and join the song,
  The multitude redeemed shall sing,
But I have drifted now so long,
  My barque to port I cannot bring;
And so I drift, with listless heart,
  Or gloomy, sighing, sad despair;
Oh, would some tear relieving start,
  But nought can move this load of care."

A WORD OF CHEER.

" Be of good cheer."

" Ho ! doubter, ho! there is relief!
  Signal the pilot, do'nt delay!
He knows the shoal, the rock, the reef,
  The channel, and the peaceful bay.
Let faith and hope now cheer thy heart,
  Bid every doubt and fear be gone,
Bid every anxious care depart,
  The night must ever yield to morn.

That Pilot knows thy heart full well,
  He knows how frail thy tossing barque,
Thy woes and conflicts he can tell,
  He knows thy voyage is drear and dark;
He'll guard thy boat through the dark sea,
  He'll speed it through the crested foam;
There is a harbor sure for thee,
  There is a glorious sunlit home.

He comes to thy relief, rejoice!
　Thy stormy voyage is almost o'er;
List to his cheery, loving voice,
　He'll bring thee to the golden shore.
What matter, if the waves run high ?
　Thoul't smile while he is at the helm;
Though they mount upward to the sky,
　They never can thy barque o'erwhelm.

The stormy tempest soon will cease,
　The clouds now break, and every star
Of hope and promise now bringeth peace;
　The beacon light shines out afar;
Oh, see the fleet approach the bay !
　Saints of all ages hear the band
Of angels singing, Come away,
　Thrice welcome to the Eden land.

Soon, soon, thoul't anchor in the bay,
　Whose silvery wavelets belt the shore,
Where golden beams amidst the spray,
　Make rainbow tints for evermore;
And thou shalt find a welcome there,
　God's own soft hand shall wipe away
Each trace of sadness, and thoul't share,
　The bliss, the joy with saints for aye."

WHAT IS NEEDED.

LUKE V. 4.

" Launch out into the deep."

Deeper water. We have been fishing too near the shore. It is no wonder that we have toiled long and caught nothing. There are plenty of fish out a little further. Launch out and drop the net. The disciples anciently had fished all night but had been unsuccessful. Their nets had gathered nothing. They had been dragging them about in shal low water. Jesus told them to launch out into the deep, and let down their nets. At his command they did so, and behold they had more fish than they knew what to do with. They called to their brothers to help them for fear that their nets would break. This lesson is

instructive. From it we may gather
some useful hints. There are many disciples to-day who have toiled long in
the master's vineyard, and are almost
discouraged, because they have caught
nothing. They have good desires and
do many good things, yet they do not
succeed in winning souls to Christ.
What is the trouble? They need to
*launch out into a deeper Christian ex-
perience.* Their religion is too much on
the surface. It does not go deep enough.
They have a mere form of godliness
without the power. In these days it
does not require much change in a
worldly person to become a member of a
church. The standard of nominal Christianity is so low that it is difficult to distinguish between those who profess religion, and those who make no profession.
If an individual sheds a few tears, rises
for prayers, he is hurried into the church,
his name enrolled, and he considered a
member in good standing, and all right
for another world; when, perhaps, the

fact in the case is, *he has not been converted at all.* There is a difference between a modern revival and an old-fashioned reformation. In ancient times men were convicted of sin. They were made to feel their lost condition. The deep and bitter sorrows of repentance pierced their hearts. Under the faithful preaching of the gospel, they were made to see that they had sinned against a holy God, and were guilty of death. They were shown the necessity of renouncing their own will, and of submitting unreservedly to the will of God. They saw that there was a wide distinction between those who served the Lord and those who served him not. They repented, they came out from the world, they put on the whole armor of God, they lived holy lives, and the change in them was marked and visible. They had a deep, thorough, Christian experience. They knew the Gospel as the power of God to their own salvation. They could tell their experience because they had one to tell. They could preach Christ, because they knew him as their personal Saviour. They were living epistles read and known of all men. They lived in the spirit, walked in the spirit, prayed in the spirit, preached in the spirit, sung in the spirit, kept the unity of the spirit, and had fellowship one with another. Such a religion as that was a mighty power among men. Sinners would tremble because God was with his people. Now, just what multitudes of professors need to-day is a deep, thorough, heart-searching, renovating, sin cleansing gospel. They need to repent to turn to God, to cut loose from the world, to consecrate all to Christ, to launch out in faith, love and obedience; trusting in God, and praying for the Holy Ghost to come down in mighty power. This done, and sinners would come in multitudes with penitent hearts, bowing at the feet of Jesus. O, let us launch out and know more of Christ, of God, and of heaven. There are heights, and depths and lengths and breadths in the love of Christ which we have not yet experienced. The Lord will do great things for his people, if they will only let him. How is it reader, do you not want more religion ? Have you not been paddling round in shoal water altogether too long? Are you not dissatisfied with your present experience ? Launch out, launch out, there is something better for you. Say with Paul, " forgetting those things which are behind, I press toward the mark for the prize of the high calling of God in Christ Jesus."

Again, might not this subject suggest the thought that some fishermen would do well to *change their fishing ground.* They have fished too long in one place. They ought to have launched out into a new field long ago. Some ministers have run in the old ruts, and preached to the same congregations for years. No great results have followed their labors. This should not be so. No minister should tarry long in a place where he is not successful. If you cannot catch fish in one locality flee to another. The world is large. Launch out into the deep. Go into the regions beyond Dont hive up in one little pen. Trust in the living God, and go where men have not been preached to death. Let down the Gospel net in faith and prayer. Be humble and willing to obey the master in all things. Go into school-houses, private houses, in groves, in tents, in mission chapels, in bethels, on ship-board, among sailors, anywhere and everywhere. Drop the net on the right side and you will be astonished at the result. Up and away. Do something. Men are perishing. Time flying. Eternity hastening. Launch out into the deep.

MORE POWER.

1 THES. I. 5.

" Our Gospel came not in word only, but in power."

More power is needed. Man is weak. He is not sufficient of himself to preach the Gospel. His knowledge is limited. Prejudice is strong. Enemies are numerous. No man can live a Christian, nor perform Christian work in his own strength. Education is good. A knowledge of the Scripture is important. An unblemished reputation is desirable. To know the truth and to be associated with good men is an advantage, but all of this is not enough to qualify a person for successful Christian service. There must be an internal work—a thorough, personal, experimental knowledge of the power of God in one's own heart. Nothing will take the place of this. All the outward fixings and equipages as useful as they may be in their place will not answer for that change which must be wrought in the heart by the power of the Holy Spirit.

The soil of the natural heart must be broken up; the thoughts, purposes, will and affections must be turned from their natural course into harmony with the will of God. It requires power to do this. No human learning or eloquence is sufficient. It must be the power that worketh effectually in those that believe." When this is experienced, then the individual may be able to exclaim with the apostle Paul, "I am not ashamed of the gospel of Christ; for it is the power of God unto salvation to every one that believeth; to the Jew first, and also to the Greek." Paul had experienced this power. He knew what he was talking about. It was not the power of truth alone—but the power that accompanies truth—the saving, cleansing, subduing, transforming power of the Holy Spirit. Paul did not prescribe for others a medicine, the efficacy of which he had not proved. He knew the efficacy, the glorious, unspeakable efficacy of the "gospel of Christ." It was the power of God unto his salvation." No wonder that he should exclaim as he did on another occasion. "This is a faithful saying and worthy of all acceptation, that Christ Jesus came into the world to save sinners of whom I am chief." He had been a great sinner, but he was gloriously saved. He thought that he ought to do "many things contrary to the name of Jesus of Nazareth," but he found that Jesus whom he persecuted was the only one who could make him every whit whole. Now, when this apostle preached, it was not with excellency of speech, or with enticing words of man's wisdom," but in " demonstration of the spirit and of power." He lived so near to God, and had such intimate communion with heaven, that those to whom he preached caught the glow of the heavenly spirit that was in him, and " became followers of him, even as he was of Christ ;" their " faith stood not in the wisdom of men, but in the power of God."

So it was with all the apostles. Men took knowledge of them that they had " been with Jesus." They were endued with " power from on high." Some of them were unlearned and ignorant men —poor fishermen, called from their boats by the sea side to follow the great Teacher, commissioned and anointed to preach the glorious gospel. It was a simple story that they told—the story of Jesus of Nazareth, but they believed what they preached, and there was such power connected with it, that hard hearted sinners wilted and fell on every side, and cried out in the bitterness of their hearts, " Men and brethren what shall we do?" Then these apostles were in their element—they knew just what to say to convicted sinners, " Repent and be baptized, every one of you in the name of Jesus Christ, for the remission of sins, and ye shall receive the gift of the Holy Ghost. For the promise is unto you and your children, and to all them that are afar off, even as many as the Lord our God shall call." This promise reaches to us—" to all that are afar off." It embraces every one who repents, and believes the gospel until the last heir of glory is sealed with the holy spirit. The Gospel must be preached with power. It must be received in power and lived in power. Paul asked certain individuals, if they had " received the Holy Ghost since they believed ?" This question we should ask ourselves. Power is needed to-day. Those who profess to be Christians need to be " endued with power from on high." We want more power in our prayer-meetings, more power in our preaching, more power in our periodicals. Give us the heavenly fire. A prominent sign of the last days was to be seen in a church " having a form of godliness, but denying the

power;" and this is apparent everywhere. The church is weak in moral
and spiritual strength, hence there are
no more conversions. O for power divine to live above sin, to overcome the
world, the flesh and the devil, and to obtain eternal victory through Him who is
the " wisdom and power of God."

GO IN FOR IT.

1 COR. XII. 31.

"A more excellent way."

God is willing his children should
have the best there is. He has made
provision for their present and eternal
happiness. We need not live on husks,
when there is plenty of corn. We need
not drink stagnant filthy water, when
there is a living spring. We need not
wear rags when there is a robe clean and
white. We need not go mourning all
the day when there is a new song we
can sing. We need not walk in the
shade when there is an abundance of
sunshine. We need not reside in Grum-
bling street, when there are plenty of
empty tenements on Thanksgiving street.
All we have got to do is to move out,
choose a better locality. Get where the
water runs, the flowers bloom, the sun

shines, the air is sweet and heavenly, the garments clean, the music joyous, the surroundings cheerful.

Put yourself where the light and love of heaven will beam all around you. Wear a smiling countenance. Be cheer. ful. Rejoice evermore. Why need you walk through the swamp where the owls hoot, and the briers scratch, when there is a high-way of holiness, where all is clear, the way straight, and the lark soaring heavenward fills the air with sweetest music? Why feed on the parched burning hill-side, when there are fertile meadows with fruits and flowers.

" Down in that beautiful valley,
Where grace crowns the meek and the lowly."

Why fret, and grumble, and repine, and wish and want, and groan, and never have, when there is peace, and joy and hope, and quiet, and rest, and salva- tion full and free for all who will accept it? You have lived at a "poor dying rate" already too long; why not give all to Christ and live hereafter at a " living rate," and shout, and sing, and rejoice all the way to the kingdom of God, and let the world see that the religion of Jesus is the best thing there is under heaven. There are a great many people trying to live religion when they have not got it. They know nothing about the light, and power, and salvation of God. They are not rooted and grounded in the truth. They are not established in the faith. They are not led by the spirit. They do not like plain, straight, old-fashioned gospel preaching. They are mere hearers of the word, and not doers. They have got a religion of their own manufacture, and what they have got is more of a torment to them than a blessing. They have left the " fountain of living waters, and hewn out to themselves cisterns, broken cisterns that will hold no water." Is it any wonder that there are no more sinners converted? The gateway of Zion is blocked up with spiritual icebergs. It is hard work to pull sinners over dead professors. Now, there is a better way to live than this. It is God's way—a blessed, holy, happy, heavenly way—a way in which you may " rejoice with joy unspeakable, and full of glory," and have within you the spirit as a well of water, springing up into everlasting life. Many have found this better way. Doubts and fears, and restlessness have given place to calm trust and sweet abiding peace in Jesus. These can recommend religion to others now, because they know its sweetness, its life, and power in their own salvation. They walk by faith and not by sight. The Lord is their sun and shield, he gives them grace and glory, and no good thing does he withhold from them, because they walk uprightly.

There is no trouble about sinners being converted, when the church is filled with the Holy Spirit. Love is the melting, moving power. If we have nothing better than the world, then in vain do we invite others to come with us. It is useless to denounce the pleasures of sin, unless we can present something far superior. This we can do if we have tasted the sweets of redeeming grace. Jesus is what men need. Present him in all his attractive loveliness. Keep self out of sight, and Jesus always in view. Sing of his mighty love. Tell others the wonders of his grace. Let his spirit fill your heart and his name be your password at the gate of every Christian temple. He is the way—the only true, the blessed, the excellent, the ever living way. Walk in him.

8

EXPERIENCE.

"We know that we have passed from death unto life."

Tell your experience. The apostles told theirs. It may have wonderful effect. One fact which a person knows from experience is worth more than a thousand arguments from mere book-knowledge. Some professed Christians have had no experience, consequently they cannot relate any. I have heard of a stranger who was travelling through the West, at one time, and it happened on a certain occasion that he was entertained at the house of a farmer. In the course of the evening their conversation turned to the subject of Christian experience. The stranger expressed a wish to hear the experience of his host. "Wife" said the farmer, " go up stairs and get a paper which you will find on one of the

beams that run across the chamber."
"My dear husband, said the wife, "the
mice ate that paper a long time ago?"
"What?" said he, "that was my experience." I apprehend that the experience of a great many is something
like this man's—when they look for it
it is not there; the mice or something
else has eaten it, or carried it away.
Now, I think that an experience in
books or papers, or an old musty manu-
script is not quite sufficient. I think
there is something better than this for
every true believer. I have heard individuals relate a long dry account of
when and where, and by whom they
were converted, and they seemed in some
measure to trust in that old, dead experience for salvation, not realizing that
it was their privilege to have a richer,
sweeter, clearer, and more heavenly
experience every day. It is well to
remember the past, and not to forget the
"way in which the Lord our God has
led us," but to trust in the past for pre-

sent salvation will not suffice. Our pathway *now* ought to shine brighter than it did when we first begun. The Christian life is not from light to darkness, but from darkness to light, not a going backward but forward, on, on, on to complete and everlasting victory. It is to know more of God, of Christ, of heaven every day. Not laying again the foundation of repentance from dead works, but going on unto perfection, growing in grace and in the knowledge of the holy scriptures. When an individual knows for himself his own acceptance into the divine favor—when he knows that his Redeemer lives—and that he has passed from death unto life—when he knows that the love of God has been shed abroad in his heart by the Holy Spirit, that he is in the Vine and the life of the vine in him, that his prayers are heard and answered—in a word when he knows that he is wholly the lord's justified, adopted, sanctified and filled with the spirit, then he can pour forth a testimony that will cut like a two-edged sword; then he can tell an experience that will be worth hearing, and that will fall with convincing power on the ears of unbelievers. O, for living, flaming, burning, melting, searching testimonies! What the world needs is a living church, baptized with holy fire from on high. Away with dead forms and lifeless ceremonies! Give us something that has salvation in it. Salvation is what men need—present salvation, living, sparkling, gushing, over-flowing, ever-abiding. Away with dry sermons, long hymns and dead prayers. Give us pith, point, pathos, enthusiasm right down old-fashioned earnestness. Give us clear, explicit, thorough, unmistakeable ever growing, never yielding experiences. We cannot live on old, mouldy, mice eaten, white bread. Give us the warm manna, right from heaven. O for a baptism of power! O for a wave of salvation to sweep over the church, and wash away everything that is unholy in Zion. O for a holy, honest ministry, and a holy liberal laity. Covetousness is a great sin. May the eternal spirit search your heart just now. Is it possible that men and women can sleep on the verge of a volcano? Up, up, my brother. Up, up, my sister, Where art thou? Are you all right? What art thou doing? Are you saved now? Others need salvation? Tell your experience.

THE CLEFT ROCK.

EXODUS XXXIII. 22.

"I will put thee in a cleft of the Rock."

" How could I bear this pilgrimage, my Lord,
　So rough, so set with trial, and with care,
Did not thy love a constant aid afford
　And prove a shelter for me every where:
A shelter that holds peace and rest within—
Even the *Rock*, once cleft to take me in.

When friends, are few and enemies are great,
　And my tired soul is forced to stand at bay,
When all the evils that had lain in wait,
　Are sudden loosed, and throng about my way,
O, then, hard pressed, I breast the powers of sin,
And turn to thee, my Rock, to take me in !

When the world's glare is rude, and I am faint,
　And one by one my hopes are withered up,
And over all sweet joys there falls a taint,
　And bitterness is most within my cup—
My stricken cry above the heat and din,
Rises to Thee that Thou would'st take me in.

And when the night comes on with darken'd sky,
　And no light breaks to show my feet the way,
I know my refuge must be very nigh,
　And night becomes as safe to me as day,
Because the voice which sounds my heart within
Says, " Lo, thy Rock is here now enter in ! "

O blessed hiding place, O safe retreat !
　My Lord, my life, how can I ever fear,
Through all the terrors of this life I meet,
　Since thy eternal presence is so near !
Give me thy grace, that I the race may win,
And through my Rock with triumph enter in."

THE MARKED SHEEP.

JOHN X. 14.

"I know my sheep."

In my boyhood days I lived at home, on a farm. Father kept a flock of sheep, I remember how my brothers and myself used to tend them; what joy it gave us to see the lambs skip and play; how we used to call them, and sometimes look after them when they had strayed away into the woods. Once in a while they would wander into our neighbors fields, and mingle with their flocks, and then we would have to separate them. This we could do without much difficulty, because each one of our sheep had a certain mark by which we could readily distinguish them, however they might be intermingled with other flocks. The mark was usually *red*, and was dyed in the wool, so that it could not easily be rubbed out, and could be seen at a distance. The process of marking them was this. About shearing time the sheep were gathered into a pen or yard by the riverside, taken one by one into the water and thoroughly washed. After the wool on them got dry they were sheaied—had their fleece cut off close to their skin. Then they were marked, and as the wool grew out again, the mark grew out with it, and could be seen wherever they went. Whoever saw them could tell whose sheep they were, by the initial of their owner's name marked in red letters on them. Now, Jesus does with his sheep what the farmer does with his. This is the process through which every one goes who enters the fold of the Good Shepherd. They are *called, washed sheared,* and *marked.* First, they are called. "My sheep hear my voice, and they follow me." He came not to call the righteous, but sinners to repentance. Far away in the wilderness of sin and unbelief he finds the lost ones and invites them to his fold. In his Gospel, by his spirit, through the voice of his ministers, he calls and says, " come unto me all ye that are weary and heavy laden and I will give you rest." " Whosoever will, let him come unto me, and him that cometh, I will in no wise cast out." All have an invitation to come. " The spirit and the bride, say come. And let him that heareth say come. And let him that is athirst come. And whosoever will let him take the water of life freely.' All do not accept this invitation. Many slight it. Those who do accept it are *washed.* It is the saviour who invites— It is the Saviour who washes. He cleanses those who come to him from all unrighteousness. He changes their hearts and renews them in spirit, and makes them new creatures. Paul has expressed what I mean in these words. " Not by works of righteousness, which we have done, but according to his mercy he saved us, by the washing of regeneration, and renewing of the Holy Ghost." (Titus, iii. 5.)   It is this inward washing that I refer to, the cleansing of the heart, the renewing of the mind.   I think too, that the primitive saints went down into the water, and were washed all over in bap-tism as an *outward token* of the *inward change*, and as expressing their hope in a future life, through a resurrection from the dead.   Much might be said on this subject, but a hint is all that is necessary Christ *shears* his sheep.   By this I mean that he *claims all they have.*   He shears off all pride, worldliness, selfish-ness, unholy ambition, love of sinful pleasure, and whatever pertains to the carnal mind.   His word is the shears, and his faithful ministers are the shearers. We are no longer our own, we are bought with a price, therefore we must glorify God in our spirit, and bodies which are his.   He claims everything, time, talent ; money, houses, lands, friends influence, education, all we have.   It is painful sometimes to submit to this shearing process, but it is necessary in order to get the *mark*, or to secure the witness of the spirit, and have engraven on us the name of the Shepherd. We must give the Lord all our bad things, all our good things—submit to all the trimming of the sharp gospel shears, until we can say with an honest believing heart;

> " Here, I give my all to thee,
> Friends, and time, and earthly store,
> Soul and body thine to be,
> Wholly thine for evermore."

How lovingly then does the good Shepherd put his mark upon us. Faith in his precious blood; secures the gift of the spirit. This is the mark by which all of his followers are distinguished, "If any man have not the Spirit of Christ he is none of his." Wherever we go and find men and women, trusting in a crucified, and risen Saviour for salvation and bringing forth the "fruit of the Spirit," these we may recognize as members of the household of faith, and heirs according to the promise. The sheep of the heavenly fold have one spirit. Down then with sectarian walls, and let the sheep of Christ worship together. Reader, have you listened to the *call?* Are you following the good Shepherd? Have you been *washed?* Are all your sins forgiven? Is your heart clean? Have you been baptized? Have you been *sheared?* Have you consecrated all to the Saviour? Are you keeping back nothing? Are you wholly the Lord's? Do those that see you know that you are a Christian? Have you the *mark?* Are you walking in the spirit? Is the mark visible? Do you know the Shepherd? "I know my sheep and am known of mine."

A CHRISTIAN.

Acts, ii. 26.

The Disciples were called Christians.

Are you a Christian? Then you are a follower of Christ. He is the founder of Christianity. His cause, though weak in the beginning, has reached an astonishing magnitude. Other systems have come to nought. Their founders were but sinful men; they passed away, and their doctrines have not reformed the lives of their followers. But Jesus lives. His cause has been a success. His teachings have reformed the lives of his followers. He has a holy people. Though he died and was buried, yet he lives as the great Head of his Church. Death hath no more dominion over him. He ever liveth and carries forward with mighty power, the cause he established when on earth. All who follow him are said to be "in him." It is a peculiar expression, yet it has deep significance. It implies a thorough change of heart, and a living vital union with him as the Source of Life. Many bear the name of christian, and are united with the church, but they are not united to Christ. There is a vast difference between being in a church, or conference, and being *in Christ*. If we belonged to a dozen churches, and were not really in Christ, it would avail us nothing. Our union with him will be evinced by the effect which it produces in our lives. If there is no change for the better, then we are deceived. We had better examine ourselves and see if our faith is one that works by love *and purifies the heart*. This is the test. "He that saith he abideth in him, ought himself also so to walk, even as he walked." Are you in Christ? or are you a christian in name only, and not in fact?

Are you a Christian? Then you are not your own. You belong to Christ.

What a person buys and pays for be-
longs to him; it is his property. If
you are a christian, Christ has bought
you and paid for you. He has placed
his seal upon you as his property. The
devil has no claim on you, and you have
no claim on yourself. Henceforth you
are not to serve satan or yourself. You
are to serve him whose property you
are. It was no mean price that He paid
for your redemption. It was not silver,
nor gold, nor precious stones. No, these
were inadequate to meet the demands
of a broken law. Had the whole earth
been a solid lump of gold, it would have
been insufficient for a ransom price.
Something more valuable than this was
required. What was it? Who can tell?
Let Inspiration answer. "Ye were not
redeemed with corruptible things as sil
ver and gold, from your vain conversation, but with the precious blood of
Christ, as of a lamb without blemish
and without spot." This was the price.
It was blood, precious blood. The

9*

blood of Jesus. O how can you serve self and the world, when it cost the Saviour his own precious blood to redeem you? How strange that christians will adorn themselves in fashionable gewgaws, and yield their bodies as instruments of unrighteousness unto sin, when, if they did but consider it, they are not their own. Christ has a claim on every part of you; your body as well as your spirit. "What, know ye not that ye are not your own, for ye are bought with a price. Therefore glorify God in your body and in your spirit, which are God's."

Are you a Christian? Then you have the spirit of Christ. "If any man have not the spirit of Christ he is none of his." Do not mistake. It is of the utmost importance that you have the Spirit, yea, it is absolutely necessary to membership in the "body of Christ." The church is his body   I do not mean that any particular local church is his body, for there are many in all the local churches who have not the Spirit; but I mean that the body of Christ is made up of all true believers the world over. All who have the Spirit belong to Christ. All true christians are members of the true church, of which Christ is Head. Do not mistake. Be sure you have the Spirit. Many will be deceived. Do not take animal emotions for the operations of the Spirit. Do not take a good natural disposition for the effects of the Spirit. Do not be satisfied with anything short of the real fruit of the Spirit. You may know by the effect it produces. If you have the Spirit, you are honest and true at all times. There is no hypocrisy in the Spirit. It is " in all righteousness, goodness and truth." Those who have it are filled with love, joy, peace, long-suffering, gentleness, goodness, faith, meekness, temperance. Wherever you see this fruit, you may know that it does not grow in nature's garden. It is the work of grace. More of this grace is needed. All profession

without this does not amount to anything.   All work without the Spirit is
mere chaff to be blown away by the
winds of the last day. Let us make sure
work for eternity The Church needs a
baptism of holy power. Sectarian walls
would then tumble to the ground.
Ministers would love each other.   The
followers of Christ would have no name
but Christian, and no creed but the
Bible. Converts would be multiplied
on every hand. The bride would get
ready to meet her coming Lord.

Are you a Christian ? Then you are
a joint-heir with Christ to an incorruptible inheritance. O wonder of wonders !
Can it be ? A poor, sinful mortal made
a joint heir with the son of God. Yes,
"The spirit itself beareth witness with
our spirit, that we are the children of
God. And if children then heirs; heirs
of God and joint-heirs with Christ ; if so
be that we suffer with him, that we may
also be glorified together." How rich,
how exalted, how secure is the Chris-

tian ! What a hope he has! This world was made for man, but through transgression he lost it. God drove him out of paradise and guarded the tree of life. Since then, sin, sorrow and death have rolled their dark waves over the human family. But Jesus came to seek and to save that which was lost. Over eighteen hundred years ago he conquered the devil, and wrenched the keys of power from the hand of death. He showed himself to his disciples, and rode triumphantly to heaven amid clouds of glory and shouts of angels. But he is coming again clothed with celestial brightness, and wielding the sword of Almighty power. At the sound of his voice ten thousand times ten thousand graves will be opened, and the teeming multitudes of the redeemed come with angel escorts to the city of the great King. All tears will be wiped away, and the last sad trace of sorrow swept from creation's brow. Old earth, so long a scene of mourning and woe, will be disrobed of the curse, and adorned with eternal beauty. The doors of paradise will be flung wide open, and the bride of the lamb welcomed to her everlasting home. The bride and the bridegroom forever united, and sharers together in the fadeless joys, and ever increasing glories of heaven. No more poverty nor want; no more sorrow nor separation; no more death knells nor heart rending farewells; no more loneliness nor longing for the presence of our Beloved; but for ever at home. He who sits on the throne shall feed them, and lead them to fountains of living water. God grant that reader and writer may share the untold delights of that beautiful world.

THE IDLE CHRISTIAN.

MATT. xx. 6.

" Why stand ye here all the day idle."

Can there be such a character ! What !
A Christian idle?   Is it possible?
Many a person no doubt, thinks himself a pretty good Christian, because, he
cannot, as he supposes, be charged with
doing anything inconsistent with his
profession.   He is guilty of no immo.
rality, and is attentive to the means of
grace.   These are good things, and all
that can be said against them is, that
they do not go far enough.   There is a
positive side to religion.   The command
is, to work in the Lord's vineyard ; and
this man does not work.   In order to
enable him to judge himself truly, let
us see what is implied in not working as
a Christian.

1st. *To be idle is to be—not like Christ.*
He worked.   He was active and indus-

trious. At the age of twelve years when found in the temple, his reply to his parents was, "wist ye not that I must be about my father's business?" From this time till he was about thirty years of age as nearly as we can gather from history, he worked as a carpenter. He, the son of the highest, did not think it beneath his dignity, to perform manual labor. When he had commenced his public ministry he said to those who gathered around him " I must work the works of Him who sent me, while it is yet day, the night cometh when no man can work" He let no moments pass by him unimproved. Read his history as portrayed in the Gospels, and see how he toiled from morning till night in public and in private, traveling, preaching and performing miracles, until at last, amidst the agonies of Calvary he exclaimed " It is finished."

2d. *To be idle is to neglect to glorify God.* Suppose you were to take a poor ragged boy from the street and adopt him into your family. After clothing, educating, protecting and befriending him you would expect a corresponding behavior on his part would you not? Certainly, you would expect him to be cheerful, loving and ever ready to obey you. Wherever he went he would glorify you as his benefactor. He would exhibit your kindness. Suppose you should plant a tree in your orchard, and after taking great pains to water, prune and cultivate it, you would expect it to bear fruit would you not? Certainly, you would expect fruit in proportion to your labor and pains and the goodness of the soil in which it was planted. Think then of your position as a professed Christian. If you are an adopted child, be cheerful and obedient. If you are a tree of righteousness remember " in this is my father glorified that ye bear much fruit."

3d. To be idle is to be false to the Church. She needs help. She is entitled to the service of all sons. There is work enough for all, all have a place and a talent for something. No person should enter the church with an idea of having an easy time, and yet how many are carried along by the efforts and influence of others, and do nothing themselves :

> " Must I be carried to the skies,
> On flowery beds of ease,
> Whilst others fought to win the prize,
> And sailed through bloody seas?"

No, no, there is only one way.

> " Sure I must fight if I would reign,
> Increase my courage Lord,
> I'll bear the toil, endure the pain,
> Supported by thy word.''

Every Christian young or old should be ready to respond like little Samuel, or like the prophet when called for, "Here am I, send me." The Church needs workers—not shirkers.

4th. To be idle is to be cruel to dy- eng souls. Suppose you should see a man in the water drowning, and made no effort to help him out, or suppose you should see a man wounded by the roadside and made no attempt to assist him would it not be awfully cruel in you to say the least? Could you do so? Would you not try, even at the risk of your own life to save a fellow-man? Yes, I believe you would. But here are men and women in more imminent peril, perishing for lack of knowledge—a knowledge of the way of salvation, perishing in a land of bibles, of churches, of ministers, of missionaries, of free schools, and Christian institutions—perishing in hovels, in cellars, in garrets, in gilded saloons, in dens of infamy —perishing in sound of church bells, in sight of home, of heaven, and eternal, glory—and perishing, because no one goes to take them by the hand, and try to win them to Christ. O, how can it be? Why are not Christians more in earnest? Let him know that he which converteth a sinner from the error of his way shall save a soul from death, and shall hide a multitude of sins."

5th. To beidle shows a lack of love. You

say you love Christ,—how do you show
it? Is it love that consists in word only?
Do you love your family? Can you sit
down in idleness and see them suffer?
No; true love will stir every nerve in
you and cause you to labor with great
delight, that you may make home
pleasant and comfortable. On the same
principle will you toil for Him who gave
his life for you. With Paul, you will
say, "The love of Christ constraineth
us. He that hath my commandments
and keepeth them, he it is that loveth
me."

*6th. To be spiritually idle is to be
spiritually poor.* Who are the wealthy
men in this world? Not those who have
wasted hour after hour in smoking, sitting around the stove, lying in bed or
loafing around shoemakers' shops or
hotels. They are those who have been
diligent in business, up, and at work,
faithfully attending to all the duties
of the farm, or store, or mill. As it is
in temporal so in spiritual things. The

person who is rich in faith, in knowledge and in spiritual graces is the one
who has been punctual at the prayer
meetings, diligent in the improvement.
of time, faithful in the performance of
every Christian duty. It is no wonder
that there are so many poor and barren
professors—they do nothing. It is the
"hand of the diligent that maketh rich."

7th.   To be idle hinders a blessing.—A
great many people desire a blessing.
They pray and wish and long for a
blessing, and yet they do not get it.
The Jews desired a blessing at one
time, and the Lord sent his prophet to
tell them how to get it. " Bring ye *all*
the tithes into the store house that there
may be meat in mine house, and prove
me now herewith, saith the Lord of
Hosts, if I will not open you the win·
dows of Heaven and pour you out a
blessing, that there will not be room
enough to receive it." Do you want a
blessing? Try this way and see if
it does not come. How can you expect

10*

the Lord to bless you while you fold your arms and do nothing. Obedience always brings a blessing. The rich young man went away sorrowful because he was not willing to do what the Saviour bid him.

8th. *To be idle is to be weak.* The boy who sells dry goods or studies hard and has no physical exercise, is weak. His flesh is soft, his muscles flabby, and he is not able to grapple with the difficulties of life, like a sunburnt sailor, or a rugged farmer, who, through constant toil, have developed their strength, and prepared themselves for usefulness. So those *fashionable* Christians, who live in the shade and feed on confectionary, fre-quent the apothecary, and the millinery, and who are so fastidious, that they can-not bear to hear an amen or a plain gos-pel sermon, and who shudder at the idea of visiting the poor—such individuals know but little of what it is to be "strong in the Lord." They are weak and helpless, so far as Christian strength and usefulness is concerned.

9th. Idleness hinders assurance.—It is no wonder that so many walk in darkness, and have no clear and satisfactory evidence that they are really accepted into the heavenly family. They are like sailors, who, neglecting to guide their vessel, let it drift away from the channel, until they get so bewildered in the darkness that they cannot see a single light house. If we would have the light of life shining on our pathway, then we must " walk in the light as he is in the light, and having fellowship one with another," we shall know by experience that the "blood of Jesus Christ cleanseth us from all sin." Giving attention to the divine directions and seeking the aid of the Holy Spirit, we shall be able to say with confident hope, " We know that he abideth in us." "Make your calling and election sure."

10th.—Idleness has no promise. No

where in the Bible is there a promise to the unfaithful. The victory is for those who overcome. The rest that remains is for those who labor. The crown is for those who run. What did the nobleman say when he came to reckon with those to whom he had entrusted the talents? To the first who had been faithful over the five, he said "welldone." To the second who had been faithful over the two, he said, "well done." But to the slothful servant, who had neglected to improve his *one* talent there was no reward. Think of this, You are not excusable, because you can do but little. He that is faithful in little, is faithful also in much. The pearly gates will be forever closed against those who have neglected to make sure an entrance there.

11*th*. *Idleness brings a curse.*—All around us, all through our land, in cities, towns and rural districts, we see the curse that follows idleness. " I went by the field of the slothful, and by the

vineyard of the man devoid of understanding. And lo, it was all grown
over with thorns, and nettles had covered
the face thereof, and the stone wall
thereof was broken down. Then I saw,
and considered it well; I looked upon it
and received instruction. Yet a little
sleep, a little slumber, a little folding
of the hands to sleep. So shall thy
poverty come as one that travelleth;
and thy want as an armed man." Once
the armies of Israel were fighting, and
certain individuals refused to come and
help. Here is what followed. " Curse
ye Meroz; curse bitterly; because they
came not up to the help of the Lord, to
the help of the Lord against the mighty."
As certainly as effect follows cause, so
certainly will the curse follow idleness.
The curse is abroa d—the curse of crime,
war, backsliding and immorality in every
form. Nothing will remove it but obedience to God.

12*th*. *Idleness is liable to a diastrous
end.*—What was the end of Sodom and

Gomorrah, whose sins were " pride, fullness of bread and abundance of idleness?"   What was the end of Babylon,
whose king made a feast to a thousand
of his lords? What was the end of Jerusalem, whose inhabitants knew not the
the time of their visitation ? What will
be the end of those who neglect the
great salvation now offered in the Gospel? Morality alone is not sufficient.
A form of Godliness will not avail.
Nothing but a character founded on
obedience to God will stand in the day
of trial. "Not every one that saith
Lord, Lord, shall enter into the kingdom,
but they that *do the will* of my Father."
Are we hearers or doers? It may be true
that you are doing nothing inconsistent
with your profession.   Is not doing
nothing almost as bad a thing as you
can do?   Any want of conformity to
the law of God is sin, as much as a transgression of it.   Be up then and doing,
work while the day lasts.

GO TO WORK.

MATT. XXI. 28.

" Son, go work to-day in my vineyard."

Why stand ye here all the day idle? Is there nothing to do? Are the sheaves all gathered in? Are the fields all reaped? Shall there be no more sinners saved? Are thy friends all in the ark? Has the Master bid thee lay down thy sickle, and cease from toil? Should you be called to give an account of your labors to-day, would you hear the " well done?" Would it be said of you, as it was of one anciently, " She hath done what she could? Have you done *all* that you could? Are you idle because you know not what else to do? Do you say that no one hath hired you? Hark! what meaneth this? " Son, go work to-day in my vineyard." These are Christ's solemn words. They express the affection of a father, and the authority of a sovereign. The fields are already white. The harvest is plenteous but the laborers are few. God loves perishing men. He has no pleasure in the death of the wicked. Go work. Tell dying men of the love of God. Invite them to Christ. Beseech them to be reconciled to God. The judgment is coming, and there is no time to be lost. Soon the work will be done. Sinners will be eternally saved, or forever lost in a little while. Oh, how can we be idle? Why are we so stupid? Up thou drowsy soldier, go to work.

> " Thy Master calls for reapers,
> And shall he call in vain ?
> Shall sheaves lie there ungathered,
> And waste upon the plain ?"

Be wise, that you may " shine as the brightness of the firmament." Turn many to righteousness, that you may dwell with the white robed throng, and wear the starry crown of eternal triumph. The resting time has not come yet.

The labor precedes the rest. Now is the working time. Be faithful a little longer. The harder the work the sweeter the rest. Think of the love of Christ. Let that constrain you. Think of the great reward. Let that inspire you. Think of the solemn command. Let that move you. It is not the hearers, but the *doers* of the word that shall be saved. Jesus says, "Go work." He says, "Go work *to-day.*" His words imply a duty, for the neglect of which, no excuse will be deemed sufficient.

There is no alternative between doing the master's work, or suffering his displeasure. O how awful it will be to suffer the wrath of God, and be forever excluded from the Holy City; yet, all who do not work for Christ must hear it said, "Depart from me ye workers of iniquity." Do you wish to escape this doom?

Are you anxious to do something for Jesus? Do you inquire *what* you are to do? *Which* is your field of labor?

When you are to enter it? How *long* you are to toil? Begin *now*, and do the best you can *right where you are.* Let me answer these questions by relating a story I once read.

"There was once a man named Quatremer Disjonval, who was thrown into a dungeon in the city of Utrecht. All alone, without a companion, without books, what could he do in a solitary prison? Apparently nothing. But unwilling to be idle, even there, he gave himself to the careful study of the habits of a spider, which had spun its web within his cell. He soon found himself able to predict changes in the weather by its movements; a trifling discovery, but yet vastly useful to him in the issue; for the next winter, a French army invaded Holland, and was in the full tide of victory, when a sudden thaw stopped its progress, and led its chiefs to resolve upon a retreat. But the prisoner, who had learned its movements from his jailor, and who, from the conduct of his spider, judged that severe frost would soon return, contrived to inform the French of his opinion. They put faith in his judgment, and maintained their ground. The frost soon returned as he predicted, the victorious French completed their conquest. Disjonval was set at liberty." ·

Here we see a man doing all that it was possible for him to do under his circumstances. It was a little thing he did, but it had mighty sequences. It determined the issue of a war, and gave him his freedom. And what does Christ require of those who labor in his vine-yard, but to do always what may be possible, under their circumstances, to diminish the amount of human sin, sorrow and suffering; and to increase human purity, comfort, and happiness? It is in our power to do many little things, which would tend to make the world brighter and pleasanter. A word, a smile, a tear, a gift, a prayer, a song, a sermon, may be the thing required, according to the ability or opportunity. Every moment is the time, every place the sphere of your labors; every human being who comes within the reach of your influence, is the subject for you to act upon. "Do good unto *all* men," is the divine injunction. The duty may sometimes seem trifling in itself, or weighty and serious; but if done in faith, and done aright, it will be fraught with mighty consequences. A virtuous act is never lost. Go work then in the spirit of this command and do "whatsoever thy hand findeth to do," with promptness and delight. Seek thy work, and it will come to thee. Perform it well, and you shall hear the "well done," when the Master cometh. Work in faith. If you see the fruit, rejoice; if not, still continue to labor, and " be not weary in well doing; for in due season you shall reap, if you faint not." The child who sows flower seeds in his garden at night is apt to weep in the morning, if the flowers do not appear. Sometimes he impatiently destroys the first labor by raking after the seeds, to see if they have not sprouted. And with a spirit similar to this do many labor for God. With zeal they sow the seed, but when the fruit delays its coming, with childlike impatience they fret and worry and pronounce their labor lost. This is wrong. It shows an undisciplined will, an unsanctified heart, and an impatience unworthy a disciple of Christ. Those who labor in the gospel field must learn to *wait*, as well as to labor. It is theirs to sow, to plant, and to water, it is God's to give the increase. The tardiness of the seed to throw out its shoots, is not always a proof that its vitality is lost. A moral harvest is often reaped after the sower has found rest in the grave. Therefore, labor in faith, and wait in hope. Bread cast upon the water shall be found again after many days. The minister who, walking in the footsteps of Jesus, "goes about doing good," may not see the immediate result of his toils;

but he has the consolation that they who sow in tears shall reap in joy. "He that goeth forth and weepeth, bearing precious seed, shall doubtless come again with rejoicing, bringing his sheaves with him." Those who work for God do not labor in vain. Their fruit will appear sooner or later, and their hearts shall be made glad. Some seed will surely fall upon good ground.

"A boy once shot an arrow into the air. So lofty was its flight, that he failed to detect the place of its descent. Long time he searched in vain around the meadow, and at last went home mourning the loss of his arrow. Years passed away. The boy became a man. After many wanderings, he revisited the haunts of his boyhood. Walking around the meadow, he gazed upon a venerable oak, whose wide spreading branches had frequently sheltered him in his boyhood, from the rays of the sultry sun. Full of old memories, he paused until his eye rested upon a feather which protruded from a hollow in the tree. He drew it forth, and with it the identical arrow which years before he mourned as lost. And is it not thus sometimes with the efforts of God's children? They speak in the ears of sinners, they bestow a tract, they utter an exhortation; or, if in the ministry, preach a sermon. They strive to watch the flight of their shaft. Vain endeavor. They cannot track it as it enters the mysterious regions of the mind, and they too often foolishly deem it lost. But it is not so. It has done its work, and either in the future years of time, or in eternity, that effort, like the long lost arrow, shall come back to the bosom of its owner, bringing with it a blessing, even the reward of a duty faithfully performed. It is said of Dr. Coke that, while journeying in America, he once attempted to ford a river, but his horse lost his foothold and was carried down the stream. The doctor narrowly escaped drowning by clinging to a bough which overhung the river side.

A lady in the vicinity gave him entertainment in his distress, sent messengers after his horse, and did him much kindness. When he left her roof he gave her a *tract !*   For five years the good doctor toiled on in the cause of God, in England and America. Whether his tract had been destroyed, or had pierced a human heart, he knew not—nay, had forgotten his gift.   But one day, on his way to a conference, a young man approached him and requested the favor of a brief conversation.

"Do you remember, dear sir, being nearly drowned in —— river some five years ago ?" " I remember it quite well," replied the doctor. " Do you recollect the widow lady at whose house you were entertained after escaping from the river ?" " I do, and never shall I forget the kindness she showed me." " And do you also remember giving her a tract, when you bade her farewell ?" " I do not, but it is very possible I did so." "Yes, sir, you did leave a tract. That lady read it and was converted. She loaned it to her neighbors, and many of them were converted too. Several of her children were also saved. A society was formed, which flourishes to this day." This statement moved the doctor to tears. But the young man after a brief pause resumed, saying: "I have not quite told you all; I am her son. That tract led me to Christ. And now, sir, I am on my way to conference to seek admission as a travelling preacher." Thus did the good doctor find his arrow in an unexpected hour. And thus will your shafts come back to you, O Christian, in due season. Courage, therefore, drooping friend; weep not over any apparent want of success. Toil on. Thy work shall be rewarded. Only labor in faith, and God's blessing will rest upon your efforts. There is much to be done. The Macedonian cry arises from every quarter, "Come over and help us!" Sinners are perishing. Death is carrying away his victims every minute, and dragging them to his dark prison-house without any hope in Christ. O how awful! Who can bear the thought of dying without a preparation to meet God? It is a dreadful thought, and yet the multitudes think but little about it. They are seeking after the vanities of the world, and neglecting the things of eternal interest. O let us do our duty. If God has saved us let us try to save others. Cry aloud and spare not; arouse the careless dreamers; thunder in their ears the truth of God; weep over the perishing; show men that you love them; be in earnest; get rid of pride and formality; plead with God until your soul is deluged with his love; then you can reach the hearts of others. It is the burning, glowing, intense love of Christ in our own hearts that makes us effectual laborers. Lazy, loafing, half-hearted professors are but cumberers of the ground. God never called men into his vineyard to *shirk*, but to *work*. Get *near* to God, and then you can get near to men. Pray for the unction from on high. God's spirit is the mighty agent. Let that fill your heart and you can be an idler no longer. You will feel for the perishing as you never felt before. O for men like Barnabas, "full of faith and of the Holy Ghost," and then we should see "much people added to the Lord." The time is short. What is done must be done quickly. Soon the last sinner will be sealed as an heir to the kingdom. The watch-men will be called to lay down their commissions at the Saviour's feet, and the gospel trumpet will be blown no more. Jesus will have ceased pleading, and sinners will be left without a Saviour, They may cry for mercy, but it will be too late. They are lost, eternally lost! All who have been faithful in the vine-yard, will then receive their reward. O how will it be with us? Shall we be free from the blood of souls? Have we done all in our power to save our fellow-men? Are we at work to-day in every way we can to save sinners? O let us resolve anew to do more for Christ than we ever yet have done. He has done great things for us. We are not our own We are bought with a price. We are the Lord's. Our time, talents, and all we possess, belong to him who hath bought us with his blood. O then let us labor cheerfully for him. The crown is before us. Only a little while, and it will be ours to wear forever. O the thought of being forever with Jesus. This is enough to stimulate us, amid all the toils and sorrows of life. Cheer up then, weary worker; be patient in well-doing; a little longer: and you will hear from the Master's lips " Well done."

YOUR MISSION.

ECCL. 9: 10.

"Whatsoever thy hand findeth to do, do it with thy
might."

" If you cannot on the ocean,
 Sail among the swiftest fleet,
Rocking on the highest billows,
 Laughing at the storms you meet;
You can stand among the sailors,
 Anchored yet within the bay,
You can lend a hand to help them,
 As they launch their boats away.

If you are too weak to journey
 Up the mountain steep and high ;
You can stand within the valley
 While the multitudes go by;
You can chant in happy measure,
 As they slowly pass along,
Though they may forget the singer,
 They will not forget the song.

If you have not gold and silver,
 Even ready to command;
If you cannot towards the needy
 Reach an ever open hand;

12

You can visit the afflicted,
  O'er the erring you can weep,
You can be a true disciple,
  Sitting at the Saviour's feet.

If you cannot in the harvest
  Garner up the richest sheaves,
Many a grain, both ripe and golden,
  Will the careless reapers' leave ;
Go and glean among the briers,
  Growing rank against the wall,
For it may be that their shadow
  Hides the heaviest wheat of all.

If you cannot in the conflict
  Prove yourself a soldier true,
If, where fire and smoke are thickest,
  There's no work for you to do;
When the battle field is silent,
  You can go with careful tread,
You can bear away the wounded,
  You can cover up the dead.

Do not then, stand idly waiting,
  For some greater work to do;
Fortune is a lazy goddess,
  She will never come to you.
Go and toil in any vineyard,
  Do not fear to do or dare;
If you want a field of labor,
  You can find it anywhere."

KEEP THY HEART.

PROV. IV. 23.

" Keep thy heart with all diligence."

The Book of Proverbs is full of good common sense. If young people would study it, instead of wasting their time in reading novels, they would find themselves much wiser and happier in time to come. Scattered through this book are many wise thoughts and maxims, which sparkle like diamonds in the coronet of a king. Would we be enriched with these treasures we must search diligently for them, and hold them with diligence when obtained. None are more precious than this: " Keep thy heart." By the heart he means the mind with all its powers—the will, the thoughts, the affections, the conscience. Keep thy heart as thou wouldst keep a *temple*. It is a sacred place. See that no unholy intruders come in there. Drive out the buyers and sellers. Cleanse the house of the Lord. Guard well the gates of this temple. Let no unclean birds build their nests on this altar. "Know ye not that ye are the temple of God, and that the spirit of God dwelleth in you? If any man defile the temple of God, him shall God destroy; for the temple of God is holy, which temple ye are." I Cor., iii. 16. 17.

Keep thy heart as thou would'st keep a *treasure.* The man who has a treasure will secure it. He puts it in a safe place to prevent thieves from carrying it away. He gets an iron safe—fire proof—with strong lock and bolts. Your heart is a treasure. It is more valuable than all the hoarded wealth of the universe. You had better lose every thing else than to lose a pure heart. But you may lose it. There are thieves all around who make it their business to steal this kind of treasure. Look out for them.

Keep thy heart as thy wouldst keep

a *garden.* It needs cultivating. Keep out the weeds. From within proceed evil thoughts. Pride, covetousness, envy, hatred, fornication, wrath, strife, fretting, murmuring, evil surmising, evil speaking, jesting, joking—all these are evil weeds and must be plucked up by the roots. In the place of them plant love, joy, peace, gentleness, long-suffering, goodness, faith, meekness, temperance,—all these are beautiful flowers, and will adorn the garden and shed forth a rich fragrance. Fence this garden and let no beasts or animals destroy its fruits and flowers. Cultivate it by study and self-examination.

Keep thy heart as a wise and experienced general would keep a besieged *garrison.* The rebels are continually on the look-out for the weakest point, where they may attack you. Do not get asleep. Watch and pray. Use the weapon of Faith. Level at your enemies the cannon of Truth. Be ever conscious of your own innocence and integrity. Put on the helmet of salvation, the breast-plate of righteousness, and use the sword of the Spirit which is the Word of God. Fortify yourself, " Stand fast, quit you like men, be strong."

Keep thy heart as thou wouldst keep a *prisoner*. The heart is treacherous and deceitful above all things. It will spring from you ere you are aware of it, unless you watch. Many persons, under certain influences, have thought their hearts under perfect control, when a change of circumstances has developed the fact that they were mistaken. Bind this prisoner with the chains of love, and perfect submission to the will of God.

Keep thy heart as thou wouldst keep a *watch*. A watch must be wound up and kept in running order. No dust must be allowed inside to clog the machinery. If it stops or runs too low or too fast, it may need cleaning, oiling and regulating. Your heart is a watch. Be sure and wind it up every day by prayer, and set it by the dial of God's word. If it needs regulating, here you will find directions how to keep it in running order, at all times, in all places, and under all circumstances. David said, "Thy word have I hid in my heart, that I might not sin against thee." "Thy word is a lamp to my feet, and a light to my path."

Keep thy heart when alone, when in company; before duty, after duty; in church, out of church; in sorrow, in joy; in prosperity, in adversity. Keep every avenue to the heart—the eye, the ear. Bolt every door. Keep out the devil. Keep Christ in your heart. Let him have it fully, completely, now and forever.

LOOKING TO JESUS.

Heb. xii: 2.

" Looking unto Jesus."

Those who run in the Christian race must have an object before them upon which to fix their attention. If we run at random we shall make crooked work and fail to obtain the prize.

I have read of a company of school boys, who one day, thought they would amuse themselves by playing in the snow. Gathering at the foot of a large oak tree, they concluded to walk across the field in diffierent directions, and see who could make the straightest path; but upon retracing their steps, it was found that only one of the boys had walked in a straight course. "Well," said the rest to Henry, "How did you do to walk so straight?" Said Henry, "Do you see that tall pine tree, yonder? I fixed my eyes on that tree, and I did not take them off till I reached the other side." Here was the secret of Henry's success. He had an object before him, and he kept his eyes fixed upon it until he had accomplished his journey.

What says the apostle to those who are commanded to " make straight paths for their feet, lest that which is lame be turned out of the way?" "Wherefore, seeing we also are compassed about with so great a cloud of witnesses, let us lay aside every weight, and the sin which doth so easily beset us, and let us run with patience the race that is set before us, looking unto Jesus the author and finisher of our faith, who, for the joy that was set before him. endured the cross, despising the shame, and is set down at the right hand of the throne of God." Heb 12: 1, 2. Ah! this is it. Looking unto Jesus. Here is the secret of success in running the Christian race. Fixing our eye on him, and forgetting the

things around and behind us, we can
" press toward the mark for the prize
of the high-calling of God in Christ
Jesus."

The word more properly signifies,
" looking off unto Jesus." Off from self,
off from the world ; off from the vanities which surround us ; off from the mis-
takes of false professors: off from sects
and parties; off from everything but
Jesus. As the disciples on the mount of
transfiguration, when the cloud of glory
had passed, looked up and saw no man,
save Jesus only, so must we turn away
our attention from all other leaders, and
be wholly absorbed in the one name,
which is above every other name, the
name *Jesus.* Jesus and Jesus only is
the one to whom we are to look for salvation. Fixing our eye on Him, how
easy it is to run with patience the Christian race. Gazing upon him, admiring
him, loving him, following him we find
besetting sins dropping off, and ourselves
becoming more and more like him. Just

as the snow and ice drop from the forest trees when the sun pours its scorching rays upon them; so will every evil thought and feeling melt from our hearts, when we stand in the full blaze of Christ's love.

There is a mighty transforming power in a steady look. Whatever we think of the most, and contemplate the longest that we become the most like The way then to be holy is to be constantly look-ing unto Jesus. Look to his cross, and find fresh motives for a closer walk with God.

> " See from his hands, his side, his feet,
> Sorrow and love flow mingled down,
> Did e'er such love and sorrow meet,
> Or thorns compose so rich a crown?"

Look to his example, and imitate his patience and benevolence. Look unto him as he stands before the throne in heaven, lifting up with ceaseless love his intercession in your behalf. He is full of sympathy and compassion. " See-ing then that we have a great high priest, that is passed into the heavens, Jesus the Son of God, let us hold fast our profession, for we have not an high priest, which cannot be touched with the feeling of our infirmities; but was in all points tempted like as we are, yet without sin. Let us, therefore come boldly unto the throne of grace, that we may obtain mercy and find grace to help in time of need." Heb. 4 : 14, 16.

In those ancient games the prize was erected upon an eminence at the end of the race course, so that those who run could see it, and be animated by it. Do we not see Jesus waving over the battlements of heaven the crown of glory? Look yonder! See how valuable it is. It is not a crown of flowers that will soon fade, but a "crown of glory that fadeth not away." Looking unto Jesus. How this helps us. In all our conflicts and sorrows, when we are tried and tempted, when we bid farewell to friends, when we are sick and lonely, when we are sin burdened and need forgiveness;

when we are in darkness and need light;
when we are weak and need strength;
when we walk through the dark valley
and shadow of death, at all times and in
all places, we can look unto Jesus. He
is ever ready to help those who look to
him. He cheers us on. "Lo, I am with
you alway." "In the world ye shall
have tribulation, but be of good cheer.
I have overcome the world." Look unto
Jesus. Believe his Word. Confess
your sins. Tell him all your troubles.

> " Can we find a friend so faithful,
> Who will all our sorrows share ?
> Jesus knows our every weakness,
> Take it to the Lord in prayer."

13

SEARCH THE CAMP.

" Up, sanctify the people."

Holiness is required. In ancient times the Lord required his people to be holy when they appeared before him to worship. " I am the Lord your God; ye shall therefore sanctify yourselves, and ye shall be holy for I am holy," Lev., xi. 45. To sanctify means to set apart for a holy purpose, to have the motives of the heart and actions of the life pure. The Israelites were not allowed to intermingle with the unholy nations around them, but they were to be separate, a holy people with whom the Almighty should manifest his presence, hence he commanded them, " Sanctify yourselves, and be ye holy. Lev. xx. 7.

When the Holy One was to speak to

the people from Mount Sinai, amid thunders and lightnings, and thick clouds of darkness, he said to Moses, " Go unto the people, and sanctify them to-day and to-morrow, and let them wash their clothes." They were to be clean, to have no impurity on their person, nor on their garments. And on every occasion afterward, when the divine presence was to be manifested in the tabernacle or in the temple, they were required to put away all that was evil in their midst, that they might come up and worship the Lord in the beauty of holiness. Nothing could be accomplished, no victories obtained, and the divine glory would not appear until they complied with the divine requirements.

When Joshua was to lead the conquering hosts across Jordan, to take possession of the goodly land, he said unto them, " sanctify yourselves; for to-morrow the Lord will do wonders among you." Joshua, iii. 5.

Purity was essential to the divine

guidance, and to their triumphant entrance into the promised Canaan. With holiness beating in their steps, and floating on their banners, they could overthrow the walls of Jericho with ram's horn trumpets, but with an Achan in the camp they were compelled to flee before their enemies, in their unsuccessful attempt to capture Ai. Do we not see a parallel to this in the church at the present time? When ministers try to rally on Israel's hosts to overcome the world, and to discomfit the enemies of truth, they too often find their arm paralyzed, their strength gone, and their enemies too strong for them. Why is it? There is an Achan in the camp. Somebody has coveted the wedge of gold and the Babylonish garment. There is sin in the church. God cannot work. Go through the camp, go through the camp. Search, search. Find out the Achan. There are lots of silver and gold hid in his tent. Dig it out, dig it out. Sanctify yourselves. Consecrate all to the Lord. Get right, get right. Confess. Strip off the old Babylonish garment. Dress plain. Examine yourselves. Search your hearts. Cleanse yourselves from all filthiness of the flesh and spirit, perfecting holiness in the fear of God. You can conquer Ai and the devil if you have the Almighty to fight your battles. Look over Israel to-day. See what conformity to the world, to its maxims, its follies, its fashions. Go into Achan's tent and see the treasures hoarded up, while God's cause languishes for want of help. The spirit of covetousness is eating out the life and power of the church. Is it any wonder that there are no more revivals of religion, no more cities captured for God? Is it any wonder that ministers pray and preach and labor until they faint, and their hearts melt as water, when Israel does not come up to the help of the Lord against the mighty. Holiness is required of the church to-day as much as it ever was. Hear Paul, the whole-souled reformer,

13*

and apostle to the Gentiles. " I beseech you therefore, brethren, by the mercies of God, that ye present your bodies a living sacrifice, holy, acceptable unto God, which is your reasonable service. And be not conformed to this world: but be ye transformed by the renewing of your mind, that ye may prove what is that good, and acceptable, and perfect will of God." Rom., xii. 1, 2. Is not this plain? Who can fail to understand this language? It is simple, and easy to be comprehended. Let us attend to this and present our bodies a living sacrifice.

Do it now. Throw away your tobacco and every other evil habit. Be holy in body and in mind. Hear him again. " Be ye not unequally yoked together with unbelievers; for what fellowship hath righteousness with unrighteousness? and what communion hath light with darkness? and what agreement hath the temple of God with idols? for ye are the temple of the living God; as God hath said, I will dwell in them, and walk in them ; and I will be their God, and they shall be my people. Wherefore come out from among them, and be ye separate, saith the Lord, and touch not the unclean thing ; and I will receive you, and will be a Father unto you, and ye shall be my sons and daughters, saith the Lord Almighty. Having therefore these promises, dearly beloved, let us cleanse ourselves from all filthiness of the flesh and spirit, perfecting holiness in the fear of God." II Cor. vi. 14–18.

READY TO PARDON.

" Thou art a God ready to pardon."

·Wonderful statement ! Glorious tidings. Ready to pardon ? Yes, *ready* to pardon. What, after I have sinned so many times, and trampled his laws under my feet? After I have resolved and promised and fallen again and again ? After I have grieved his tender spirit, crucified his son afresh, and brought reproach on his cause? After I have been turned out of church, and my brethren have lost confidence in me? Is it possible? Can it be so? Will he pardon *me*? Is he ready to pardon me *now*? Yes, he is waiting and watching for your return. He is able to save to the " uttermost " all who will come to him. Just as you are, you may come, and come now,

" All the fitness he requireth,
Is to *feel* your *need* of him."

Are you ready? He is ready and waiting. Do you ask for evidence? See it in the *provision he has made for the exercise of pardon.*

Behold the Lamb of God stretched on yonder cross! What does it mean? Is he dying to atone for his own sins? No, I find no fault in this man," was the statement of the Roman Judge. He was holy, harmless and undefiled. No guile was ever found in his mouth. Why is it then that he endures such agony, and dies such a painful death? Ah! sinner, this is all for thee. "God hath made him to be sin for us who knew no sin, that we might be made the righteousness of God in him." He commendeth his love toward us, in that while we were yet sinners Christ died for us." All we like sheep have gone astray, we have turned every one to his own way, but the Lord hath laid on him the iniquity of us all." Can you doubt his willingness to pardon?

See it in the *invitations of his word.*

Would you invite your friends to come and dine with you if you did not love them, or were not ready or willing to receive them. Think not then, that God is trifling when he sends his invitations to you. Listen to him now, and see if he is not ready to pardon and to feast you upon his bounties "Come now and let us reason together, saith the Lord. Though your sins be as scarlet, they shall be as white as snow; though they be red like crimson they shall be as wool." Again, " Ho every one that thirsteth, come ye to the waters; and he that hath no money; come ye, buy and eat; yea. come, buy wine and milk without money and without price." What are these invitations for? Do they not unfold his readiness to pardon? Is not this encouragement for all to come? Who need stay away with such invitations as these sounding in his ears ?

See it in the *examples of his pardoning mercy.* Some of these have been the chief of sinners; sinners of long standing; sinners whose crimes have not only been numberless, but attended with every aggravation. You have read of Manasseh; of the dying thief; of the murderers of Christ; of the Corinthian converts: yet all these obtained mercy! Vile, wretched, and miserable as these were, they found pardon. Have you read of Peter, who denied his master? He was pardoned. Have you read of Ma. ry Magdalene out of whom were cast seven devils? She became a meek fol. lower of Jesus. Have you read of Saul, who held the garment of those who killed Stephen? He was the " chief of sinners," yet he obtained pardon and was made the " chief apostle." Sinner, there is hope for you. Jesus can save to the ut- termost. You may have gone down deep, deep into sin, but there is one able to save you. Only trust him. He is ready to pardon. " Yes, sinner, he is a God ready to pardon : *but mark these thoughts.*

He is ready to pardon only those who *repent.* Show me a single scripture

where the bestowment of the one is un-
connected with the exercise of the other;
Manasseh found pardon; but it was,
when he humbled himself before God
and repented. Paul found pardon; but
it was when he stopped sinning and
turned to the Lord. Peter found pardon;
but it was when he remembered his sin,
and wept tears of contrition. Jesus came
not to " call the righteous, but sinners to
repentance." " Repent ye, therefore and
be converted, that your sins may be
blotted out." If we confess our sins,
He is faithful and just to forgive us our
sins, and to cleanse us from all unrighteousness." " He that covereth his sins
shall not prosper, but he that confesseth
and forsaketh them shall have mercy."
Are you sorry for your sins? Have you
confessed them, and asked for pardon?
Will you forsake them for ever?

He is ready to pardon but *only in this
life.* There is no pardon beyond the
grave. Those who hope for pardon by
delaying an application for it till the close

of life will make a great mistake. If we fail to obtain pardon in this world, we need not look for it in another. Some teach that there will be a chance for repentance in a future age, but such teachings are not warranted by scripture. *Now* is the accepted time. *To day* is the day of salvation. *Now* we can make sure of pardon; to-morrow it may be too late. Now the door of mercy is open; to-morrow it may be shut. "When once the master of the house is risen up, and hath shut to the door, and ye begin to stand without, and to knock at the door, saying, Lord, Lord, open unto us; and he shall answer and say unto you, I know you not, whence ye are: depart from me ye workers of iniquity." No pardon *then.* Now, he is ready to pardon. Reader, are you pardoned? Have you repented of your sins, and had them forgiven through faith in the blood of Christ? Are you conscious of this? Have you the evidence hat follows pardon? Are you justified? Have you

peace with God ?   Have you the Spirit?
Are you walking by faith ?   If so, go on.
Live above sin.   Watch and pray that
you enter not into temptation.   If you
are not pardoned I beseech you to repent
this very day.   Turn to God with all
your heart.   Put it not off.   You have
no time to spare.   The Lord is calling
you to-day.   He is ready to pardon.
"Seek ye the Lord while he may be
found; call ye upon him while he is
near.   Let the wicked forsake his way,
and the unrighteous man his thoughts,
and let him return unto the Lord, and
he will have mercy upon him, and to our
God, for he will *abundantly pardon.*"

DOWN BRAKES.

ACTS, VIII. 38.

" He commanded the chariot to stand still."

There is danger ahead. When I was a school-boy I remember of reading a story about the burning of a railroad bridge, and how a train loaded with passengers was prevented from plunging into the awful chasm. A little boy by the name of Eli, discovered that the bridge was burned, just as an express train was nearly due. He saw the danger and knew that unless the train could be stopped there would be a fearful loss of life. Stepping on to the track he saw the train coming under full headway, and, with hat off and both hands uplift-ed, he ran towards it right in the centre of the track, screaming at the top of his voice, " The bridge is burned ! the bridge is burned!" The engineer saw him and blew the whistle for him to get out of the way, but at the risk of his own life he still ran toward the engine crying, "The bridge is burned! the bridge is burned!" The whistle blew again for "down brakes," and the train was stopped just in time. The passengers came out, and after viewing the danger, loaded the little boy with presents, and showered kisses upon his cheek. By his forethought and courage, he had saved them from an awful death, and saved many homes from weeping and wailing.

Sinner, there is danger ahead. There is an awful chasm into which you will shortly be plunged unless you stop. You do not see it. With the thoughtless, pleasure seeking multitude, you are crowding the halls of mirth, swearing, smok'ng, drinking, dancing, carousing, and little dreaming of danger, while the train of Time is speeding you on with fearful velocity toward the awful preci- pice. I see your danger. With pen and

voice, and uplifted hand, I would cry
with all my might, stop, stop; the bridge
is burned., the bridge is burned. The road
you are travelling is not safe. The train
you are in will not take you into the Celestial Depot. You are on the direct road
to perdition. Stop. Down brakes, down
brakes. Abate your speed. Stop. Stand
still. Look ahead. See where you are
going. Let me explain what I mean.
There is an awful judgment day just
before you. The word of God declares
it, and that can never fail. " Rejoice, O
young man, in thy youth ; and let thy
heart cheer thee in the days of thy youth,
and walk in the ways of thine heart, and
in the sight of thine eyes ; but know
thou, that for all these things God will
bring thee into judgment." Eccl., xi. 9.
Do you wonder that I ask you to stop?
How can you sin in view of that awful
day? It is certainly coming. Listen
again. " God now commandeth all men
every where to repent. Because he hath
appointed a day in the which he will

judge the world in righteousness, by that man whom he hath ordained, whereof he hath given assurance unto all men, in that he hath raised him from the dead." Acts, xvii 31. Do you wonder that I am in earnest when I ask you to repent? Are you not surprised that I am not more in earnest? I am in earnest. Would that I had a tongue of fire, and a voice of thunder that I might warn the world, and rescue thousands from eternal death. The Lord is in earnest. He is not willing that you should perish. He is long suffering, not wtlling that any should perish, but rather all would come to repentance. But you must submit to his terms. He offers pardon and eternal salvation to all who will repent and believe the gospel. He has sent out his ministers to give the alarm,—to call upon men every where to repent; to warn the world of the judgment to come. They are watchmen on the walls of Zion, and are to give the signal when they see danger ahead.

Woe to them if they are unfaithful. Woe to you, if they give the warning and you heed it not. O sinner, stop, stop, Go no further in sin. I warn you this day in the name of my Master to stop. O I beseech you to turn unto God this day. Repent of your sins. Cry to the Lord for pardon. Flee to Jesus whose blood can cleanse you from all unrighteousness. Pray as you never prayed before. Read the Bible—ask for the Holy Spirit to illuminate your heart. God will save you. O think of the glories of heaven. There is a crown for you. Will you have it? O delay not. Time is flying. The judgment is coming. We shall soon be there. Stop. Pray.

RETURNING HOME.

"Repentance toward God"

Repentance not *away* from God, but *toward* God. Consciousness of guilt causes man to escape, if possible, the Divine presence. True repentance brings him back to acknowledge his guilt. When Adam had sinned, he tried to hide himself amid the trees of the garden, but the Lord saw him and called him forth to give an account of himself. It is the same with us to-day. When we have gone astray from the right path, and are conscious that we have transgressed the commandment of our heavenly Father, we feel a shrinking from his presence, a reluctance to meet him in prayer, a disposition to hide and get away where our guilt will not be exposed. This is a wrong way and a vain attempt. We cannot hide from God. We may escape the notice of our fellow men, and sometimes get beyond their reach, but we cannot escape the all-searching glance of Him whose eyes are in every place, nor elude the grasp of Him who holdeth the universe in his hand. The right way is to *come directly to God and ask his forgiveness.*

There are many who repent but they repent in the wrong way. They are sorry, but still they wander further and further from home. True repentance *turns a person around*, and sets his face *toward* his Father. The history of the prodigal son illustrates true repentance. He went far away from home into a foreign land, and there spent his substance in riotous living, with proud and gay companions. As long as his money lasted he had plenty of associates, and a splendid time in sinful pleasures. After awhile there came a money-panic. Business was dull, fields did not yield their crops, and there was a famine in the land. He began to be in want. Times looked exceedingly dark. He tried to get employment but could not. By and by he went and joined himself to a citizen of that country, who sent him into his fields to feed swine. This must have been very humiliating, but it was this or nothing. Starvation stared him in the face. "He fain would have filled his belly with the husks which the swine did eat, and no man gave unto him." Friendless and alone, ragged and almost starved, he sat down and wept. O how glad he would have been to see his good old mother, or his gray-headed father! He thought of home, but he had been such a wild, wicked boy, that he feared he would not be received. He knew not that his dear old father still loved him, and was watching for his return. At length he came to himself, and said: "How many hired servants of my father have bread enough and to spare, and I perish with hunger! I will arise and go to my father, and will say unto him, Father, I have sinned against heaven, and before thee, and am no more worthy to be called thy son; make me as one of thy hired servants. And he arose and came to his father." Slowly across the fields he comes, with bowed head, and a sorrowful heart. Ah, there is no pride about him now. He is very humble. He has learned a few excellent lessons in deep affliction, and is willing now to be even a servant, if his father will only accept him as such. But look yonder! I see his father going to meet him. When the returning one was " yet a great way off, his father saw him, and had compassion, and *ran* and fell on his neck, and kissed him." They weep together. O what a meeting is this!—A lost son meeting his loving father. The son begins to tell his story: "Father I have sinned"—the father stops him. "Bring forth the best robe and put it on him, and put a ring on his hand, and shoes on his feet. Bring hither the fatted calf, and kill it; and let us eat, and be merry;

for this my son was dead, and is alive again; he was lost, and is found. And they began to be merry."

Backslider, you are the prodigal. God is your father. He loves you still. You have wandered far away. Stop now. Arise and go home. Your father is look-looking out for your return. He has eyes of mercy, feet of mercy, hands of mercy, lips of mercy. He will meet you on the way. Repent—repent—repent. Confess your sins. Do not starve in a foreign land. Your friends still love you. They want you to come back. Jesus waits to wash all your sins away. O say this very moment "I will arise and go to my Father." Return—return. Get out of this desert of sin, and go home. Heaven will be glad at your return.

"Come weary wanderer, cease thy toilsome
    straying,
No longer seek for peace where none is found ;
Come, and thy Saviour's gentle voice obeying,
Find here thy home where love and joy abound·"

THE DESERT ROCK.

1 Cor. x: 4.

" They drank of that spiritual Rock that followed
them, and that Rock was Christ,"

" Rock of the desert, pouring still,
Thy stream the thirsty soul to fill;
  Rock of the desert, now as full,
  Of living water, pure and cool,
    We stand beside thy stream.

Rock of eternity, to thee,
In thirst and weariness we flee;
  Thy waters cannot cease to pour;
  Their fulness is for evermore;
    Let him that thirsteth come.

Bright water of eternity,
We come, we come to drink of thee.
  The voice of welcome that we hear,
  The voice dispelling every fear,
    Is " whosoever will."

River of life, upon thy brink,
We sit, and of thy waters drink;
  The murmur of thy sparkling wave,
  Speaks still of Him who came to save,
    Who bids us drink and live.

River of peace, so full and bright,
Each drop, clear shining with the light;
  And still the voice that comes from thee,
  The voice that telleth all is free,
    Is—" whosoever will."

River of love, so deep and wide,
All heaven is in thy flowing tide;
  For all the love of God is here,
  The love that casteth out all fear,
    The " whosoever will."

River of God, still flowing on,
Thy source the everlasting throne.
  River of Heaven, translucent stream,
  Thy fullness ever at the brim,
    For—" whosoever will."

River of health, thy current pours
Its freshness on these leprous shores !
  Pure Jordan, bidding all draw nigh,
  For health and immortality,
    With—" whosoever will."

Dear river, what a sun is thine!
What glories on thy waters shine!
  What freshness in each sparkling drop,
  And still the voice that cometh up
    Is—" whosoever will."

SECRET PRAYER.

MATT. vi. 6.

" Enter into thy closet."

The Christian will have a place for secret prayer. By this he is distinguished from the time of his conversion. He delights to be alone with God. As the fish cannot live out of its native element—water, so the christian cannot live out of his native element — prayer. Whatever his engagements, or situation, or circustances, whether on laud or sea, in the city, or in the country, the true christian will find some place where he can retire occasionally and commune alone with his Saviour. Rob him of this privilege, and you rob him of his joy and strength. Like Sampson shorn of his locks, his strength is gone. Jesus himself felt the need of secret prayer.

Frequently he retired from the crowd, got out of the bustle and confusion of the city, and went away to the fields and mountains to pray. Sometimes he continued all night in prayer. He does not require us to do what he did not do himself. He has taught us to pray in secret, both by precept and example. All Bible characters, noted for piety and devotion, have had a time and a place for secret prayer. David said, " Morning, evening, and at noon will I pray and cry aloud, and the Lord shall hear my voice. It is a good thing to give thanks unto the Lord, to show forth his loving kindness in the morning, and his faithfulness every night." Daniel went into his chamber and prayed three times a day, and he was not afraid of others hearing him, for he prayed with the windows open. Ezekiel went forth into the fields, and there God talked with him. Peter prayed on the housetop. Paul and Silas in prison. Lydia by the river side. None have wanted for time

or a place when they have really thirsted
for communion with God.

> " Where'er we seek him he is found,
> And every place is holy ground."

They who feel the need of Divine
guidance and commit their ways unto
the Lord, will find the promise ever
true—"As thy day is so shall thy
strength be." Retirement prepares the
christian for all other duties. Said
Judge Hale, in his letters to his children, "If I omit praying, and reading
a portion of God's blessed Word, in the
morning, nothing goes well with me all
the day." Dr. Boerhaave said that his
" daily practice of retiring for an hour
in the morning, and spending it in devotion, and meditation, gave him firmness and vigor for the business of the
whole day." It is in secret that the
minister best prepares himself for the
discharge of his duties. Tarrying at
the throne of grace until he is endued
with power from on high, he comes forth

15*

like a giant, able to conquer his enemies,
and to lead on the armies of Truth to
sure and complete victory.   David never
would have dared to go out and fight
Goliath, had he known nothing of secret
communion with his God.   It was in
the wilderness that he had been trained
for public service.   There unnoticed by
the world, he had found the source of
abiding strength, and from the sheep-
fold he came to slay the giant of the
Philistines, and lead on to final triumph
Israel's retreating hosts.   He was a cho
sen man—a man after God's own heart;
and why ? Because he could say, "Whom
have I in heaven but Thee ? and there
is none upon earth that I desire beside
Thee."   The Lord was his portion, his
rock, his salvation, his strength.   He
communed much with his God, and became God-like.   We soon assume the
manner, and imbibe the spirit of those
with whom we are familiar, especially
if the individual be a distinguished per.
sonage, and we pre-eminently revere

and love him.   Upon this principle, the more we have to do with God, the more we shall grow into his likeness, and " be followers of him, as dear children." When Moses came down from the mount his face shone; and although he was not aware of the lustre himself, the people could not steadfastly behold him for the glory of his countenance, and he was constrained to hide it under a veil. The christian, too, may be insensible of his excellences and proficiencies, but his profiting will appear unto all men ; all will take knowledge of him that he has been with Jesus.   Do you pray in secret ? Have you a place where you go each day and pour out your desires to God ? Says good Mathew Henry, " Backsliding begins at the closet door." How is it with you ? Do you take as much delight in secret prayer as you did once ? Remember the words of Jesus.   Enter into thy closet.   Do it this very day.

A WEEPING WORLD.

"Jesus saw her weeping."

This is a weeping world. Once it was not. The time will come when there shall be no more weeping. When the morning stars sang together, and all the sons of God shouted for joy, there were no tears. Earth was then sinless. Man was placed in Paradise. Around him everything was pure, lovely, and beautiful. No sin had defiled his heart, no curse blighted the earth. God, looking upon all things that he had made could say "it is very good." Man was the noblest of all beings created of dust. He was endowed with a mind capable of obeying his Creator or of disobeying him. The test came. Adam yielded to temptation. The flood gates of iniquity were opened. Sin, with its long train of misery and sorrows, came in. Earth was cursed. Tears began to flow. Since then this once beautiful world has been a vale of tears, a land of mourning, of the dying, and of the dead. Man has struggled with the weakness of his own nature, and fought bravely for the victory over those unseen influences, which have sought his ruin, but failing oftentimes, has wept and realized the need of One "mighty to save." The hope of a better state of things has given him courage, and been the mainspring of action in all his endeavors to lead a pure life, and to attain that perfect and immortal inheritance promised in the unfailing word. Faith in a coming One has inspired him to exercise his utmost energies in overcoming the world, and has produced a quiet spirit of submission under those disappointments, and chastening afflictions, which he could not avert, and which it was necessary that he should have in order to be a partaker of divine holiness, and be fitted for eternal association with sinless beings. God will yet have a holy world and a holy people. The work of reconstruction is going on. It will be completed by and by. Out of the ruin and chaos of this revolted planet shall spring to view a new earth of indescribable grandeur and incomparable loveliness. Out of the wreck of fallen humanity, shall be gathered a pure, blessed, redeemed, glorified multitude, to associate for ever with the inhabitants of heaven in Paradise restored.

Earth and heaven shall yet be blended in beautiful harmony. Divinity has been linked with humanity. Christ having taken human nature with him to heaven, will also exalt *human* beings to sit with him on his throne, and to share the glories of his everlasting home. What a prospect is this! Well can we afford to toil, and sacrifice, and suffer, and weep, a little while here, if such a high destiny awaits

us over there. Are we chastened? It
is a loving hand that smites us. He doth
not grieve nor afflict willingly the children of men, but it is to separate the
evil from us, to purify our hearts, to
wean us from a world that would lure us
to ruin, to draw our affections heavenward, that he destroys our earthly idols,
and lays desolate the pleasant objects in
which we trusted. It is blessed to weep.
What a relief it affords us when the
heart is over-burdened with sorrow, and
the bosom swells with inexpressible
grief, to go away alone and give vent to
our feelings in floods of tears. When
we feel sad, sin-burdened, and lonely,
how blessed it is to weep. The worst kind
of grief is that which lies heavy on the
heart and cannot find expression through
tears. Those who are penitent and
broken-hearted do not carry their burdens long, for they wash them away
with their tears. " Blessed are they
that mourn for they shall be comforted."
It is blessed to weep with those who

weep.   How sweet to kneel beside the penitent one, and weep with him as he mourns over his sins.   How comforting to the bereaved to have some one come and weep with them. Human sympathy is valuable. It helps to heal the wounds in the sorrowful heart. When Martha and Mary wept over the loss of their brother, many of their friends came to weep with them.   It seems that they had many friends, but O, there was one precious loving friend, who could sympa· thize with them as no human being could. It was Jesus. He saw them weeping; he knew their sorrows, and he came and wept with them. O, what comfort there is in the thought that Jesus is our friend. He sees, he knows, he sympathizes with us in all our sorrows. He is touched with the feeling of our infirmities. In that future world there will be no more weeping, "for the Lamb which is in the midst of the throne shall feed them, and shall lead them unto living fountains of water: and God shall wipe away all tears from their eyes."   Rev. vii: 17.

THE GRAVE.

Job xvii. 13.

"If I wait the grave is mine house."

Where are the dead? Some say "in heaven," some say "in hell," some say "in purgatory," some say "in the spirit land." But what says the bible? To the law and to the testimony, if they speak not according to this word it is because there is no light in them. Where did Abraham put Sarah when she had died? . "Abraham buried Sarah his wife in the cave of the field of Macpelah, before Mamre; the same is Hebron, in the land of Canaan." What was done with Abraham when had died? "Then Abraham gave up the ghost, and died in a good old age, an old man, and full of years; and was gathered to his people. And his sons Isaac and Ishmael buried him in the cave of Macpelah." Gen. xxv. 8, 9. In this ancient family burying ground the patriarchs were buried. Jacob said to his son Joseph "Lo I die ; in my grave which I have digged for me in the land of Canaan, there shalt thou bury me." Here Joseph wished to be buried, and he said to the children of Israel, "God shall surely visit you, and ye shall carry up my bones from hence." Jacob and Joseph did not wish to be buried in Egypt. As the time of death drew near they thought of the old family burying ground, and there they wished to sleep in unconscious repose. When Job the patriarch of Uz, thought he was about to pass away he exclaimed: "O that thou wouldst hide me in the grave, that thou wouldst keep me secret, until thy wrath be past, that thou wouldst appoint me a set time and remember me." And again, "I know that thou wilt bring me to death, and to the house appointed for all living." His affliction was so great that he saw no chance to recover. But God was merciful and turned his affliction into joy. Yet this wa only a *reprieve* from *immediate* death. So Job understood it, and though for a time his life was prolonged and he was blessed more abundantly, yet said he, "If I wait the grave is mine house." However rich or prosperous in life, all he needed at last was some little spot of ground in which to be buried. With this accord the words of Solomon, "All go unto one place ; all are of the dust and all turn to dust again." From the dust man was created, dust he is called while living, and unto dust must he return when he dies. What have we then, to be proud of? The great, the good, the noble, the learned, the benevolent, the beautiful have died. Patriarchs, prophets, apostles, martyrs, saints, young, and old, rich and poor, have all met in death's great reception room—the grave. However proud we may be of our beauty, or wealth, or relatives, titles, or position in society, here we must part with all.

We brought nothing into this world,
and it is certain that we can carry nothing out.

"How loved, how valued once avails thee
not ; to whom related, or by whom begot; a heap
of dust alone remains of thee; 'tis all thou art and
all the proud shall be."

The grave may be considered as an
universal receptacle. Though the me-
morials of death do not every where
meet our eye, and particular places are
properly appropriated for interment,
and some of them are very capacious
and crowded; yet there is scarcely a spot
that holds not some portion of humanity.
Perhaps some one has been turned to
dust beneath the very place where you
are now sitting.

"What is the world itself ? Thy world ?
A grave. Where is the dust that has not been alive?
The spade, the plough disturbs our ancestors. From
human mould we reap our daily bread. O'er devas-
tations we blind revels keep. Whole buried town's
support the dancer's heel. As nature wide our
ruins spread; and death inhabits all things, and will
until the coming of the son of man."

If the grave is an universal receptacle,

then how *painful its separations.* It severs the tenderest ties—thy father, thy mother, thy sister, thy brother, thy wife, thy husband, thy child, thy friend. Who has not some spot the dearest on earth, and rendered sacred by a deposit more precious than gold.

Yonder goes a mother to weep for her child, and a child to weep for its mother. Death draws his dividing line through all circles. Who has not sustained some bereavement? We are related to the dead as well as to the living. "Lover and friend hast thou put far from me, and mine acquaintance into darkness."

Then how *personal the claims of the grave.* Can *I* escape it? If it be appointed for all living, surely it will require me. Yes, it will require me. I cannot escape it. I may escape a thousand other things that befall my fellow-creatures; but I must follow them here. I see in *their* end, the emblem, the pledge, the certainty of my own. No privilege can exempt me here. I am going the

way of all the earth. I may die soon.
I may live a few years, yet " *if I wait
the grave is mine house.*" Solemn thought.
But the grave to a christian, is a sweet
resting place until the morning of glory
dawns. It is the dress chamber in which
he puts on his beautiful garments, to
arise and meet his Lord in the air. But
to others, it is the cell of condemnation
in which the malefactor is lodged till he
is led out to punishment." They that
sleep in the dust of the earth shall awake,
some to everlasting life, and some to
shame and everlasting contempt." Dan.
xii. 2. What will be your destiny beyond the grave ?

THE RISEN JESUS.

MARK XXVIII. 6.

" He is risen."

" He is risen." This presupposes that he was *dead*. That cannot have a resurrection which is not dead. If Jesus never died then the statement concerning his resurrection is not true for that can only *re live* which has been once alive and is now dead. Jesus was once alive. He went about doing good. The world was moved by his power. He was taken by wicked hands and nailed to the cross of Calvary. After a few hours of suffering, he said " It is finished," and he gave up the Ghost, or breathed his last. The Son of God was dead. A Roman soldier with a spear pierced his side There was no life in him. Joseph of Aramathea begged his body and laid it in his own new sepulchre. A great stone was rolled to the door and sealed, and the grave was guarded by a band of soldiers.

"He is risen." This is a *fact established*. Angels declared it. Those holy beings can never tell that which is not true. On the morning of the third day, an angel rolled away the great stone and sat upon it. Hear what he said to the women who had come to embalm the Saviour's body: "Be not affrighted. Ye seek Jesus of Nazareth who was crucified: he is risen; he is not here: behold the place where they laid him." The empty sepulchre confirmed the angel's statement that he was *alive*.

O, hasten and tell the tidings ye faithful women. Jesus is alive. Tell his disciples that you have heard the angels, and seen the empty tomb. Tarry not, go quickly.

"He is risen." *The disciples saw him.* He showed himself alive after his passion by many infallible proofs.

An unbelieving world has never seen a risen Jesus. They beheld him for the last time when he hung upon the cross. But the disciples saw him and associated with him after his resurrection. He showed his hands and his feet. He ate and drank with them and convinced them that he was the very same Jesus. He confirmed the faith of doubting Thomas, and renewed the commission of fallen Peter.

"He is risen." *Then he is the Son of God.* All doubts vanish now. This settles the question of his divinity. Skeptics and infidels may ground the weapons of their rebellion here. God would not have raised him from the dead if he had not been his Son. No chance for evasion now. Jesus is the true Messiah. "He was declared to be the Son of God with power, according to the Spirit of holiness, by the resurrection from the dead." This demonstrates his divinity.

"He is risen." Then the *justifi-*

cation of believers is secured. " He was delivered for our offences." We had offended God. The law was against us. The awful condemnation of a guilty conscience was sinking us. The debt was more than we could pay. But Jesus takes our place. He meets the demands of the law. He dies the just for the unjust. " He was raised again for our justification." This settles the account. We are now in the hands of Christ. He has bought us and we belong to him. " Being justified by faith we have peace with God through our Lord Jesus Christ."

"He is risen." Then the *holy spirit is given to his people.* This was the " promise of his father." It could not come unless Jesus went away. " If I go not away the Comforter will not come, but if I go away I will send the comforter." Precious promise. It has been fulfilled. We have received the Comforter, and we know that Jesus lives. The spirit and the word agree.

"He is risen." Then *they also which sleep in Jesus will be raised.* He has conquered death and broken the fetters of the grave. He is the "pledge," the "earnest," the "first fruits" of them that sleep. "But now is Christ risen from the dead, and become the first fruits of them that slept. For since by man came death, by man came also the resurrection of the dead." Blessed hope! Glorious truth! "I would not have you to be ignorant, brethren, concerning them which are asleep, that ye sorrow not even as others which have no hope. For if we believe that Jesus died and rose again, even so them also which sleep in Jesus will God bring with him. For this we say unto you by the word of the Lord, that we which are alive and remain unto the coming of the Lord shall not prevent them which are asleep. For the Lord himself shall descend from heaven, with a shout, with the voice of the archangel, and with the trump of God : and the dead in Christ shall rise first . Then we which are alive and remain shall be caught up together with them in the clouds to meet the Lord in the air: and so shall we ever be with the Lord. Wherefore, comfort one another with these words."

"He is risen." Then he will *establish his kingdom and reign forever.* · Thus, it is written, "He shall be great, and shall be called the son of the highest; and the Lord God shall give unto him the throne of his father David, and he shall reign over the house of Jacob forever; and of his kingdom there shall be no end." "I saw one like the son of man come with the clouds of heaven, and there was given him dominion, and glory, and a kingdom." "And the kingdom, and dominion and greatness of the kingdom under the whole heaven, was given to the people of the saints of the most high."

Are we risen to walk in newness of life? Set your affections on things above.

JOY IN THE MORNING.

Psalm xxx. 5.

" Joy cometh in the morning."

Joy cometh in the morning. This is true in our daily experience. Night is the season for rest. Many a tired laborer comes home at night weary and fretted with the cares of the day. He may have met with disappointments in business; some one may have wronged him; he may have been irritated and said things which cause his heart to feel sad, or from some other cause he is not as happy as he might be when he comes home to his loving family. It is best not to say much to him, for he is nervous and needs rest. After reading the scripture and offering prayer he retires, but for a time he is restless on his pillow. By and by sweet sleep comes, and he forgets all his

17

troubles. He awakes. It is morning. The sun is lighting up the eastern horizon; the birds are singing their joyful notes, the air is refreshing; the flowers are sending out their sweet aroma, and everything seems new. He goes out, and really the morning is so delightful he catches an inspiration of joy. He feels like a new man. He sings, and enters upon his day's work with renewed courage. Joy cometh in the morning. See the children yonder, going to school. How they run, and skip, and laugh, and sing. They are happy and joyful. At night it was not so. They came home fretted with their lessons, peevish, and somewhat sorrowful. Father and mother had to caress them, and put the tired little creatures to bed. A few hours of refreshing sleep drove away all their troubles. Joy cometh in the morning, and they are out again, cheerful and active, plucking the wild flowers, washing their feet in the dew on their way to school, where with renewed vigor they engage in their studies. It is blessed to behold the morning light after watching with the sick. The hours of night drag slowly by as you sit near the sick friend or dying child. The monotonous tick, tick of the clock, or the mournful chirp, chirp of the cricket, makes you feel as if it would be joyful to see the sunbeams creeping in at the window. Joy cometh in the morning. How cheering it must be to the sailor boy after encountering a storm at sea, amid darkness and tempest, with shattered rigging, splashing sea-foam, and fear of a lea-shore—to see the sun beaming through the clouds, assuring him that the storm is past, and the morning come again. The watcher on the deck, the soldier on the battle-field, the traveller in the forest all know the joy that cometh in the morning. The season of conviction for sin is a dark and sorrowful night. The person who is awakened to see his lost condition out of Christ does not feel much like singing or dancing. Music for a time has lost its sweetness.

Joy departs. Love for mirth and merriment is gone. Friends cannot comfort. He sees himself a lost sinner. Sorrow rests down upon his heart. He tries to pray, but O how dark every thing appears! His conviction grows deeper. He seeks solitude and wishes to find relief to his burdened heart. He prays, "Lord save or I perish." Light breaks into his mind. By faith he beholds the Lamb of God. The sinner is forgiven. He seems to hear a sweet voice saying, "Thy faith hath saved thee, go in peace, and sin no more." O what a morning is this! It is the morning of forgiveness. He is filled with joy and thanksgiving. He goes to his friends and says, "Come all ye that fear God, and I will declare what he hath done for my soul." Joy is manifestative. It is stirring—full of music, and activity. Joy cometh in the morning. This world is now in its night season. Sin abounds, sorrow and tears flow. Death enters our homes and robs us of our loved ones.

It is a night of weeping. The cries of mourning float on every breeze.

"The air is full of farewells to the dying
And weepings for the dead.
The heart of Rachel for her children crying
And will not be comforted."

Darkness settles over the land—moral darkness—the darkness of sin, of ignorance, of unbelief, of crime. The church weeps. From death-beds, from secret places of prayer, from scenes of suffering and distress, voices are heard saying, " how long O Lord, how long?" From afar they cry to the watchmen on Zion's walls, " Watchmen, what of the night? watchmen, what of the night?" The watchmen send back the response as they see the tokens of approaching day, " behold the morning cometh." It is the morning of eternal joy. See yonder through the rifted clouds the mountain peaks of the better land. The distant hills and forests are tinged with the golden glory of morning. The eastern sky is crimson with the beams of dawn.

ing day.   Mourner cease your weeping,
morning cometh.   See streaks of glory
shining through yonder grave-yard.   It
is the morning of the resurrection, the
morning of eternal glory. Then shall
the "ransomed of the Lord return, and
come to Zion with songs and everlasting
joy upon their heads : they shall obtain
joy and gladness, and sorrow and sighing shall flee away."   Isa. xxxv. 10.

HOME RELIGION.

2 SAM. VI: 20.

" Then David returned to bless his household."

How can a Christian bless his household? This is an important question. We suppose here that he *has* a family. He is not a poor, illiberal, solitary individual; preferring vice, or mopishness or an escape from expense, and trouble, to a state which was designed to complete the happiness of Adam in Paradise, and which Inspiration has pronounced to be "honorable in all." He believes in the wisdom and veracity of God, who has said, "It is not good for man to be alone," and having "children as olive plants around his table," he will endeavor to bring them up in the "nurture and admonition of the Lord," believing that if he "trains them in the way they should go, when they are old they will not de-part from it." So David thought and acted. Official duties did not cause him to neglect his family. "Then David returned to bless his household."

If you are the head of a family you may bless your household by *Example* It is natural for the soldier to look to his captain, the scholar to his teacher, the servant to his master, the child to his parent. Superiors are watched. How you live, the example you set, has a controlling influence over those under you. It will amount to but little for you to require your household to walk in the right path, unless you walk there yourself. Children are imitators; they do what they see others do. Do not for-get this.

You may bless your household by *Government.* Order is heaven's first law. All of God's arrangements are harmonious. Every thing in a family should be in order. Your meals, your devotional exercises, your rising, and your rest. It is important to peace, to health, to diligence, and economy. What strife, and misery, and poverty there is in some households, just because there is no order, no regularity. Chil dren eating at all times a day, clothes scattered about the floor, chairs turned up side down, the doors slamming, and everything in general confusion. Have order. If you are the head of the family, *be* the head. Give the commands and have them obeyed. Train up a child in the way that he *should* go, and not in the way that he would. For what is Abraham commended? "I know him, that he will command his children and his household after him, that they shall keep the ways of the Lord to do justice and judgment." What was the resolution of Joshua? "As for me and my house, we *will* serve the Lord." He had a will in the matter. Do not forget this.

You may bless your household by *Instruction.* Study good books and papers on various subjects. Get your head full of the right kind of knowledge. Some parents do not know much of anything. They live in ignorance, and bring up their children the same. I suppose there are many homes in this enlightened country, where there are not half a dozen good books in the house. You should be able to instruct your children in those things that pertain to the health of their bodies, as well as to the purity of their minds. Watch close their secret habits. Know where your children go, know what they read, now with whom they associate. Evil communications corrupt good manners. Do not forget this.

You may bless your household by *securing their attendance on the means of Grace.* How strange and inconsistent it looks for parents to attend church, and allow their children to stroll about on the Sabbath. Early impressions and practices are not soon forgotten. Take them with you to the house of God, and let them hear the word of truth proclaimed. Ministers ought to preach sim

ple enough so the children can understand them. Do not starve the lambs
to death, nor drive them away by scold-
ing at them. Give them something to
eat. In your deep researches after truth,
and eagerness to present it, do not forget the lambs. Jesus did not. He took
them in his arms and blessed them, and
in his last charge to Peter, he said, "Feed
my lambs." Do not forget this.

You may bless your household by having family *Devotion.* Read the Bible, and
pray with your family. Serve God at
home. Let your home be a pure, sweet,
heavenly place. Make it attractive. Be
pleasant, good natured, and heavenly
minded. If there is anything beautiful
and lovely in this world, it is a christian
home, where parents and children live
in peace and harmony, and where the
Son of Peace continually abides. Give
your children music. Sing praises to
Jesus. O fathers, O mothers, whatever
your engagements in other directions,
do not forget your homes. Whatever

else you neglect, do not neglect your family. Bring up your children in the nurture and admonition of the Lord. You are responsible. If you want your children to rise up and bless you through eternal years, then "bless your household" while you have health, time and opportunity. Do not forget this.

RIGHT AND WRONG.

PROV. IV. 26.

" Ponder the path of thy feet."

Walk with your eyes open. See where you are going There are a great many dangerous paths in this world.   It is almost impossible for a young person to start out from home, without being led into some wrong path. There are snares, temptations, and a thousand voices, inviting in the wrong direction. Look well, consider every step you take. Wrong beginning, makes wrong ending. Be sure you are right, and then go ahead. If you were going on a long journey it would be of the utmost importance that you got into the right train.   Many a man who has made mis-takes, would retrace his steps and take a different course if he could.   It is too late.   He is shipwrecked for eternity.

18

Failures in business, failures in health, failures in happiness, failures of heaven, are often to be attributed to wrong beginnings. There *is* a right way. See that you choose it.

Suppose two sea captains are about to sail to some foreign port. One of them is wise the other unwise. We may suppose them to reason after this manner. One says, " the voyage I am about to take across the ocean is a long and perilous one. I will prepare for it. I will have my vessel overhauled, repaired, and everything made sure and strong as possible, so that she may be able to stand any storm, and take my cargo safely to the distant port." He does so. At considerable expense and pains he makes due preparation for the voyage. He goes to the custom house officer and gets his clearance papers, and is all ready to hoist sail and away. The other captain makes no preparation of this kind. He says—" my old craft has made many successful voyages. I cannot go to the expense and trouble of having her overhauled. I know she needs repairing, but I will risk it."

He loads her. He does not go to the custom house officer to get his clearance papers. He is presumptuous and runs the risk of entering a foreign port without any legal documents to show who he is or where he is from. All is ready, and they sail. Down the harbor they go. One apparently bids as fair to make as successful a voyage as the other. They sail on. By and by they get out into the ocean, where the mighty winds and waves test the strength of each vessel. One rides on majestically cutting her way through the foam, showing no signs of leakage, and giving her captain and crew no uneasiness concerning her safety. The other snaps and creaks, and tosses about in a fearful manner. The captain and crew are frightened, and work night and day at the pumps to keep her from sinking. The recklessness of this captain has caused them a great deal of trouble, but this is not the worst of it. After a while the distant port heaves in view. They approach the harbor and cast anchor. An officer is sent off to inspect the vessels, and to call for the papers of each captain. The first shows his clearance papers, and gives satisfactory evidence that everything is all right. He is permitted to pull up to the wharf, discharge his cargo, buy and sell, and is protected by the authorities. The papers of the other captain are called for. He has none to show. "Who are you? where are you from?" says the officer. He has nothing to show. He and the crew are taken and bound as prisoners. The vessel and cargo is taken, and perhaps sold or anchored near to some fort where the enemies guns are levelled at it. This captain came to a miserable end. He had a perilous voyage, and when he reached the other side was captured, lost his vessel, cargo and perhaps his own life. These captains may illustrate the conduct and destiny of two classes of men. The wise and foolish, or those who start *right* and those who start *wrong* on the voyage of life. The wise man says: "I am destined for another world. I am going to a distant port. I know that my voyage will be attended with perils. I shall need strength to meet the diffi·culties. I shall also need something to recommend me at the end of my journey. I will prepare for it. I will overhaul my heart and get all sin out of it. I will repent and amend my ways. I will go to the throne of grace and get my clearance papers, signed by the Lord Jesus Christ."

The foolish man says, "I know that I cannot always live here. My judg·ment tells me that I am sailing on towards the great future, but then I guess it will be well enough with me. I cannot fuss and bother about repentance and holy living. I think I will come out about as well as the best of them. I will risk it." He does not repent, pray nor believe in the Lord Jesus as the Saviour of sinners. A few years pass on. They come to the judgment seat. The officers of heaven are sent out to examine them. "Where are your papers?" "Here they are," says the wise man, "sealed with the blood of Jesus." "Well done, thou good and faithful servant," says the officer "thou hast been faithful over a few things, I will make thee ruler over many things, enter thou into the joy of thy Lord." The face of the foolish man gathers paleness, and he hears the words, "Bind him, hand and foot and cast him into outer darkness."

WHICH KIND OF RELIGION.

JAMES I. 27.

" Pure religion and undefiled before God and the Father is this: To visit the fatherless and widows in their affliction, and to keep himself unspotted from the world."

We read of three kinds of religion in the Bible. "*Our* religion," "*vain* religion," and "*pure* religion." Which kind have you? We may learn something of "our religion," as to its nature and effects, by glancing at the character of the apostle Paul previous to his conversion. He says concerning himself, that "after the straitest sect of our religion I lived a Pharisee." How did he live? He gloried in his literary attainments, his strict adherence to the law, his pedigree as being a literal descendent of Abraham, and no doubt like many Pharisees he made long prayers, and gave tithes of all that he possessed. But he had a narrow, bigoted, hateful, sectarian, persecuting spirit. *Our* religion was all the religion he thought good for anything, and he wanted to kill and exterminate those who advanced views contrary to the *law*, though they manifested a much better spirit than the sect to which he belonged. He held the garments of those who killed Stephen, and he was on his way to Damascus to persecute the saints when the Lord met him. He was so hateful that the Lord had to knock him off of his horse, and smite him with blindness before he would yield. He thought our religion must be supported, even if he killed all the good people on earth. I wonder if there is any of this kind of religion in our day? Are there any long-faced churchgoers who are all wrapped up in "our party"? Are there any sectarians? Are there any persecutors? A thorough conversion to God set Paul all right, and it will do the same for others.

The next is "vain religion." How shall I define what this is? I think I will let James do it: "If any man among you seemeth to be religious, and bridleth not his tongue, this man's religion is vain." How much of this kind there is in the land! Go to yonder prayer meeting; hear that brother or sister sing, talk, and pray; surely they must be saints. Follow them home; how they scold and fret, and find fault. See them go through the neighborhood; what tattling, whispering, backbiting, slandering, gossiping, and evil speaking. That unruly member does run like a wild horse without a bridle, and the whole community is soon in an uproar. Perhaps there is no one point where professors are more liable to fail than in an improper use of the tongue. Remember that for "every idle word we speak, we must give account thereof in the day of judgment." Jesting, joking and all corrupt and evil speaking is positively forbidden. Do not forget it. If any man among you seemeth to be religious, and bridleth not his tongue, this man's religion is vain." He is deceived. If you are sailing on this course stop. Tack ship and sail in another direction.

The third, is "pure religion." This is the right kind. How heavenly it is! This kind will take you into the celestial port. Let James speak again. "Pure religion and undefiled before God and the Father is this: To visit the fatherless and widows in their affliction, and to keep himself unspotted from the world." This religion is pure in its origin, pure in its nature, pure in its influence. It purifies and elevates every heart into which it enters. It improves society wherever it touches it. It has stamped upon it the benediction of heaven, for it is "pure and undefiled before God the Father." No person can have this kind of religion unless he is made better. t destroys the old selfish disposition, and implants a spirit of benevolence. It uproots the carnal mind which tends to death, and produces the spiritual mind which is life and peace. This religion does not live pent up within itself; it gushes forth, leaps out, like a spring overleaping its banks and spreading its life-giving waters all around. O for more of this kind of religion. How many poor widows and orphans would be relieved of their sufferings. How much money would be appropriated to a better purpose, which is now expended for needless and distasteful apparel. How many precious moments would be saved or improved in cultivating the mind, which are now wasted. How holy and heavenly would the prayer meeting be. With what delight and power would ministers preach if the truth was received into good and honest hearts. Do not forget. There are three kinds of religion: Our religion Vain religion, Pure religion. Which kind have you?

LIGHT IN THE BINNACLE.

1 JOHN I. 7.

" Walk in the Light."

" Box the compass" is an expression sometimes used by mariners when they are about to take a sea voyage. Now the compass is one of the most important instruments used in sea-faring business. Without it no captain would dare venture on the trackless ocean, for he would not know which way to steer, and his vessel would be in constant danger of striking rocks, reefs or sand-bars.

But the compass with its needle, ever pointing to the north is placed in a little box called the binnacle near the wheel, so that the man who steers the vessel can keep his *eye upon it*, and thus know in which direction to turn the helm. The compass would be of no importance to the helmsman unless he could *see* it. A blind man could not steer a vessel, neither can a man with good eyesight, unless the compass is placed where he can see it, and know exactly which way its needle points. In order to do this there must be *light in the binnacle*. Man cannot see in the dark—he must have light. But the ocean is traversed quite as much in the night as in the day. When the shades of evening gather over the deep, a lamp is placed in the side of the binnacle, so as to throw light on the compass. Thus the helmsman can guide his vessel just as well in the night as in the day. Men are sailing on life's ocean. All are voyagers—either to the port of everlasting rest, or to the gulf of everlasting perdition. None are standing still—all are being rapidly borne on to one place or the other. The Bible is the compass by which all are invited to steer. It always points in the right direction. But in order that men may steer their lives by this compass they must have *light*. This is a dark world. Men must in some way be enabled to see the points of the compass or they cannot steer in the right direction. The Holy Spirit is the light. Men may have the Bible in their hands. and a knowledge of it in their heads, and yet not *see* its truths, nor steer their lives by it. Their minds are not lit up by the Spirit. They have no faith They are yet carnal. They are blind through unbelief. They need the illumination of heaven in order that they may understand the truth, and see to steer their vessel towards the celestial port. The same spirit that inspired holy men to write the Scriptures, will light up the mind of every individual who reads them with a believing heart. A great many are sailing on, on, on toward eternity, and yet they are sailing in the dark. Some ministers are sailing in the dark. They preach not the word of God, and they have not his spirit. They are blind leaders of the blind. Churches are sailing in the dark. They have beautiful church edifices, beautiful pulpits, beautiful gilt edge bibles, beautiful choirs, beautiful forms and ceremonies, beautiful congregations—but no spirit, no light. All church members who have not the spirit are in the dark. More light, more light! Light in the binnacle is what they need. More spirituality, more heavenly mindedness, more activity and earnestness in prayer-meetings. Not lightning flashes, but steady, burning, light. The world of unbelievers is in the dark. Sailing on to the great and awful gulf of eternal destruction, with no light. Unbelief, unbelief! This shuts out the light of God. It is the office of the spirit to give light. It is the spirit that convinces of sin, of righteousness, and of a judgment to come. It is the spirit that leads into all truth. The natural man discerneth not the things of the spirit. They are foolishness unto him. How can he un.derstand the bible when he grieves the spirit and shuts out of his mind the light of heaven?   All work without the spirit is work in the dark.   Awake, thou that sleepest, and Christ shall give thee light.   Light in the binnacle! light in the binnacle!   Prayer is the match that lights the lamp in the heart.   When the captain wishes a light placed in the binnacle, he rings a bell to call the steward.   Voyager to eternity, have you asked for light that you might see to steer your vessel in the channel of *obedience*?   Ring the bell of prayer Ring, ring, call for light.   "Ask and ye shall receive."   Thank God, some have light in the binnacle.   They see the truth, and are walking in the spirit—sailing sweetly on toward the heavenly port. Soon they will anchor safe within the vail.

A BROTHER'S ADVICE.

GEN. XLV. 24.

" See that ye fall not out by the way."

Who can read the history of Joseph and his brethren and not have their heart stirred within them? It is one of those touching narratives that moves upon our feelings, and leaves an impression that we cannot soon forget. Every part of this account is interesting ;· but I only wish now, to call your attention to the advice Joseph gave to his brethren when he sent them away from Egypt, with Pharoah's orders to bring back their father, Jacob, with all his family. From it we may draw some useful lessons for our practical improvement. Joseph had long ago discovered his brethren to be of a peevish, quarrelsome disposition, and the late very moving transaction of his making himself known unto them, he justly imagined would call to their minds what they had formerly done unto him, and very probably be the occasion of reviving their mutual contentions; and that which confirmed him in the suspicion was his overhearing his eldest brother upbraiding the rest on this head, saying, " Spake I not unto you saying ' do not sin against the child, and ye would not hear? therefore behold, also his blood is required.' " Gen. 42. 22. Though at that time they knew not that he understood them, because he conferred with them by an interpreter.

Upon so well grounded suspicion, then, no advice appeared to him more seasonable or necessary to be given them at parting, than this caution, " See that ye fall not out by the way."

Joseph still loved his brethren, and had forgiven them all, and therefore lays them all under the same obligation to love and forgive one another. The same charge our Lord Jesus Christ hath given to all his disciples, that they "love one another," that they "live in peace," and that they "forgive as they hope to be forgiven." Let us notice—

1st. That this exhortation to avoid all uncharitable contentions does not oblige us to be of the same sentiments, or in the strict sense of the phrase, to think the same thing. This, in the very nature of things is simply impossible. There are probably no two individuals in the world that see and think exactly alike in all things. Whilst men are of a different make and complexion of mind, they must see things differently, and hold different opinions. And to compel men by acts of violence to be of the same opinion, is infinitely absurd. To use harsh means and torment men's bodies in order to enlighten their minds, is just as reasonable as to pretend to cure a wound by an argument; and they who are for informing men's judgments by breaking their bones, may as well attempt to set them again by a lecture on logic.

No; as men are accountable for their own conduct, they should think and judge for themselves, and not suffer their consciences to be domineered over, or their understanding dictated to, or their faith directed, by any man or any set of men, any further than their directions and instructions harmonize with the words of the great Teacher.

One is your Master, even Christ, and all ye are brethren. To His words we are required to give heed; for the words that he hath spoken shall judge us in the last day.

2d. In order to live in peace very large and charitable allowances must be made for every one's *natural tempers*; which, though it be not so much out of his power as his judgment, yet as it is natural and born with him, it is one of the most difficult things in the world some-times, to correct its faults, and though reason directs and religion obliges us to this, yet how often does *nature* rebel against reason, evade religion, and break through the restraints of both. Whatever abatements are due on this score, certain it is that as persons may be of different judgments, so they may be of different *natural dispositions* and yet be united in the bonds of Christian love.

3d. This exhortation does not require us to be insensible to the mistakes and feelings of good men. All men are encompassed with infirmities, and are liable to mistakes. In the best of men we may see things that appear to us to be wrong, and we cannot help being displeased therewith, and the more in proportion as we ourselves are affected thereby. But with all their faults we ought to love them for their virtues, at least the latter should prevent our falling out with them on account of the former. One great object of the adversary is, to persuade people to magnify the faults of others while they diminish their own. Backbiting, faultfinding, and evil speak-

ing, are prevailing sins among professors
of religion at the present time.   We can
hardly go into any public place but what
we hear professors talking about the
faults of some absent brother or sister.
Is this right? Does God approve of conduct which is not in harmony with his
word? Are we to treat an erring brother
or sister as boys do a football; every
one give it a kick, and send it further as
it passes along? Are we to drive individuals away from the right path, instead
of *winning* them to it? Is this not one
reason why so many churches, that were
once united, have been divided and their
members scattered? I think it is.   Brethren have allowed envy, malice, and
hatred, to creep into their hearts; consequently there is " confusion and every
evil work." The wisdom that is from
above is first pure, then peaceable, gentle,
and easy to be entreated, full of mercy
and good fruits, without partiality, and
without hypocrisy.   And the fruit of
righteousness is sown in peace of them

that make peace. It is true we are not to wink at sin, nor fellowship those who persist in doing wrong; but if a brother or sister be overtaken in a fault, are we to reject them, speak evil of them, and shun their company? Let the Apostle answer. "Brethren if a man be over-taken in a fault, ye which are spiritual, restore such an one in the spirit of meek-ness; considering thyself, lest thou also be tempted." Gal. 6. 1.

Irreconcilable resentment is not al-lowed to Christians. The whole extent of the duty recommended in the lan-guage of Joseph to his brethren may be comprehended under the great Christian duty of *love*, so often inculcated and re peated in the New Testament. This is the very genius and spirit of the Gospel, without which there can be nothing of the true Christian disposition. Of this the apostle Paul gives a most beautiful and animated description, in (1 Cor. 13.), under the name of Charity. He says, "Charity suffereth long, and is kind;

charity envieth not; charity vaunteth not itself, is not puffed up; Doth not behave itself unseemingly, seeketh not her own, is not easily provoked, thinketh no evil; Rejoiceth not in iniquity, but rejoiceth in the truth; Beareth all things, believeth all things, hopeth all things, endureth all things. Charity never faileth."

The relation and circumstances which Joseph's brethren were in when he gave them this advice, and which were so many inducements to them to comply with it, are in a good degree common to us, and so far are equally proper to engage us to the same. For

1st. We are Brethren. Like the patriarchs we have all one Father. We should therefore love as brethren.

All believers were once children of wrath, walking in darkness, hateful and hating one another; but they have been redeemed from sin, and adopted into the family of God. Now they are no more strangers and foreigners, but fellow citizens with the saints and of the household of God. Among brethren there is oftentimes a great dissimilitude of condition and circumstances. Some are weak, others strong. Some excel in capacity, others in good temper; others in knowledge; but that which should unite all in affection is, that they have all one Father. As we are all children of our Father in heaven, and are taught to acknowledge and address him as such, this filial relation wherein we stand to God, should remind us of the fraternal relation wherein we stand to one another, and the mutual love it requires. " Love as brethren ;" be " kindly affectioned one to another, with brotherly love; " let brotherly love continue."

2d. It was another considerable motive to the patriarchs to comply with this advice, that it was given them by their own dear exalted brother, who had not only the tenderest regard for their welfare and interest, by the ties of nature, but was able to support it by the power and dignity of his station. We have the same motive to influence us; for this commandment to "love one another," is given us by Jesus Christ himself, who is not ashamed to call us brethren, and "who was in all things made like unto his brethren, that he might be a merciful and faithful high priest in things pertaining to God, to make reconciliation for the sins of the people." And as our exalted Brother, who having loved his own, he loved them unto the end, he hath given us this reasonable advice, that we "love one another, as he hath loved us;" and by this, says he, "shall all the world know that ye are my disciples; if ye have love one to another."

3d. Another reason why Joseph's brethren should not fall out with one another was, *because they were all guilty*, not only in their behavior towards Joseph, but in all probability in their behavior towards one another. And is not this our own case? However, most certain it is we are all no less guilty towards Christ, than Joseph's brethren were towards him. We stand infinitely more in need of his forgiveness than any of our offending brethren do of ours, and his readiness to forgive us all should strongly induce us to forgive one another. Therefore this duty may be further urged from this consideration, that we all hope to be forgiven of God. And our forgiving others is made one of the express conditions of our receiving forgiveness from him. We pray on no other terms, when we say, "Forgive us our trespasses, as we forgive them that trespass against us." And our Lord explains that petition of his prayer in this sense: "If," says he, "ye forgive not men their trespasses, neither will your Father forgive you your trespasses." And to induce us to this forgiving temper, no consideration can have a greater force than this, that our greatest enemy cannot stand so much in need of our forgiveness as we do of God's. So Joseph's

brethren knew when they came to their
father's house, they should be all filled
with self-remorse and shame, in unravel-
ing to him the whole mystery of his
son's story, and would all want his forgiveness, which consideration would be
a strong argument to comply with their
brother's advice—" Not to fall out by
the way."

4th. Like them we are all *sojourners
in a strange land.*   It has been observed
that there is not here to be found a more
sincere and disinterested friendship than
among those of the same country in foreign lands, at a distance from their common home.   Their being exposed to the
same hazards, difficulties, and disasters,
and having the same interests, views,
and designs with regard to their journey, is that which knits their hearts
together with a more than common tie
of affection.   Happy if the same observation could with equal force be made
of all Christians who, in a religious view,
are in the same circumstances,—pilgrims

and strangers on the earth, having no continuing city here, but seeking one to come. It is something unnatural and unscriptural, then, for them to be alienated in their affections, and to increase the inconveniences of their journey by their "falling out by the way."

5th. Another circumstance common to us with Joseph's brethren, and which should equally induce us to comply with the exhortation he gave them is, that we are all traveling to the *same home;* that whatever different subordinate views we may each entertain here, our main view is the same; we are all tending to the same place. Our Father's house, where there are many mansions, the holy Jerusalem, the "city which hath foundations, whose builder and maker is God." Jacob's sons were going back to their father's house; So all Christians are traveling toward the same home. What a glorious home that will be, where the saints of all ages shall meet. How beautifully the beloved John has described

20*

it in Rev. 21 and 22. Our Elder Brother
will send forth his angels, and purge out
of his kingdom all things that offend
and them which do iniquity; then shall
the righteous shine forth as the sun in
the kingdom of their Father. This
blessed hope of what we expect to enjoy when we arrive safely at home, should
effectually prevent us from "falling out
by the way." The world to come will
be a place that knows nothing of those
jarring discords, feuds, and confusions,
which infest this sinful world. That
will be a peaceful country. The strifes
and bickerings of time will be done, and
the weary pilgrims who have been tossed
and buffeted in a foreign land, will then
find rest and peace near the throne of
God. Then the Prince of peace will
reign, and those that "wait upon the
Lord shall inherit the earth, and delight
themselves in the abundance of peace."
Sin shall be banished from that peaceful clime. Sorrow and sighing shall flee
away. The angels shall gather his elect

from every land, and they shall sit down in the kingdom with Abraham, Isaac, and Jacob, and go no more out forever.

Let us, then, remember the home towards which we are rapidly hastening, and it will be a good incentive to prevent our "falling out by the way."

THE MIND OF JESUS.

PHIL. ii. 5.

" Let this mind be in you."

Jesus was *Humble*. No proud, vain, swelling thoughts of self importance, ever found a place in his mind. If he had been a depraved, sinful mortal, doubtless he would have been " puffed up" through the wonderful success attending his ministry; but he was the Son of the Highest, hence, he needed not to seek glory among men. He certainly had occasion to glory after the flesh, had he been so disposed, for his position was higher than the angels, and his power mightier than the kings of the earth. With a word, he could hush the raging of the sea, and quiet the fury of the tempest. He could cast out devils, and heal all manner of diseases; he could raise the dead and banish the gloom of the grave; he could feed the hungry multitudes with a handful of bread; he could foretell future events, and read the hidden thoughts of the human heart. Never was there a character before like him. In him were hid all the treasures of wisdom and knowledge. He was the only begotten of the father— full of grace and truth. Surely if pride were commendable, such a being as this would have exhibited it in his life and conversation; but no, behold the humility of Him—" who being in the form of God, thought it not robbery to be equal with God; but made himself of no reputation, and took upon him the form of a servant, and was made in the likeness of men. And being found in fashion as a man he humbled himself and became obedient unto death, even the death of the cross" Let this mind be in you which was also in Christ Jesus. He did not seek for a great name, a great position or to be thought well of before men. He did not flaunt and

make a great display with costly apparel.
He was satisfied with plain and common
things.   His was an every day religion.
The common people heard him gladly,
and to the poor he preached the words
of everlasting life.   Everywhere and on
all occasions he manifested a meek and
lowly spirit, and it was upon the humble
that he pronounced his benediction.
" Blessed are the poor in spirit for theirs
is the kingdom of heaven." Have we
the mind that was in Jesus ?   Have we
come to him and received of his spirit ?
Do we imitate him in meekness and humility ?

Jesus was *Bold*. Humility is not
laziness, neither is boldness brass.
There are many who manifest a brazen-
faced audacity; they fear neither God
nor man; and they rush on through the
world trying to make others think they
are good or great when they are not.
This was not the boldness Jesus manifested.   His was a boldness based upon
right principles, right motives and right

doing. He knew that he was right; hence he could meet his enemies with unblushing confidence. He could rebuke iniquity and expose hypocrisy, and put to shame and silence those who came to catch him in his conversation. Looking in the face of the Pharisees, who persecuted, and sought to take him, he could say, "which of you convinceth me of sin?" Jesus had a consciousness of purity within; hence he moved onward with unyielding and unflinching courage through his earthly career, despising the shame until he experienced the last act of human indignity in being nailed to the cross. He did not fail or become discouraged. He had a work to do and he *did* it. He triumphed over all his foes, and became the captain of our salvation. Have we this mind? Are we bold for Jesus? Do we confess him before men? Can we stand for God though we stand alone?

Jesus was *Patient.* His life was one of toil, of suffering, of conflict, of perplexity, of persecution, of temptation, of sorrow and of tears. He was a man of sorrows and acquainted with grief; yet no murmuring or repining ever escaped his lips. The storm gusts of earth never raised a ripple upon the placid waters of his mind. In him all was calm, clear, serene and tranquil as a midsummer sunset. There was nothing hasty, impetuous or fretful about him. He was self-possessed. In patient, lamb-like submission he received the scourge and the crown of thorns No feeling of anger or revenge rankled in his bosom. Even amid the darkness and solemnity of Calvary's tragic scenes the rainbow of peace hung about his gentle brow. Was there ever patience like his? "When he was reviled he reviled not again; when he suffered he threatened not, but committed himself to him that judgeth righteously." Have we this mind? Are we patient under the provocations of life? Do we never murmur nor repine? Are our minds calm and clear as a waveless stream? Do the muddy waters of strife and envy never rise to the surface? When disappointments come are we calm then? When adversity approaches can we kiss the rod? When loved ones are snatched away by the hand of death are we quiet and submissive? When laid upon a sick bed do we calmly trust in our heavenly father? Do we take pleasure in infirmities, and rejoice in the midst of earth's keenest sorrows? It is given unto us in the behalf of Christ, not only to believe on his name, but also to suffer for his sake.

Jesus was *Benevolent.* In him there was a fullness of love, sympathy, compassion and goodness. It was impossible for him not to do good—it was a part of his nature. From his heart and hands flowed a constant stream of blessings. He was rich, yet for our sakes he became poor, that we through his poverty might become rich. Gaze upon him, yonder by the temple gates,

as the rays of the setting sun fall upon
him.   He has toiled all day, and still is
ready to toil all night if need be.   See
the multitude throng him, bringing the
halt, the lame, the maimed, the blind,
and the sick of every description.   How
he heals and blesses them all and asks
not a penny.   How he forgives the penitent, binds up the broken hearted, and
bids the captives go free.   How gently
he reproves the erring and restores the
fallen.   O, was there ever love like the
love of Jesus?   What has he not done
for the comfort and salvation of sinners?
He gave his life for hi enemies.   Have
we this mind ?   Are we benevolent ?   Is
it our chief delight to do good ?   Do
we *deny self* to bless others ?

Jesus was *Holy*.   He was born holy,
but this holiness was maintained by a
strict conformity to his Father's will.
He was obedient in all things.   There
were no rebellious thoughts in his heart.
His language was—"I delight to do thy
will, O God; yea thy law is within my

heart." He loved to keep his Father's commandments. His obedience was cheerful and affectionate. Have we this mind? Are we holy? Have we been transformed by the renewing of our mind? Do we delight to obey God? Are we obedient in *all* things? Only the obedient have the promise of eternal salvation. May we have the mind of Jesus.

FORGIVENESS:

Matt. vi. 12.

" Forgive us as we forgive."

Does it read just so ? Yes, Just so. Turn and read it. Does it mean just so ? Just so exactly. If you do not from your heart forgive men their trespasses, then it is useless for you to ask forgiveness of God. The ground on which we may expect forgiveness of our heavenly father, is that we forgive those who have trespassed against us. Now, if we come to the throne of grace to offer prayer and supplication, and there, remember that we have aught against any person on earth, and we cannot freely, fully and *from the heart* forgive *them*, then we need not hope for forgiveness from Him against whom we have sinned so many times, for the Saviour has taught us to pray after this manner " forgive us our trespasses as we forgive those who have trespassed against us." Note that little word " as ; " *as we forgive.* This little word has great power in this connection. It is the point on which the success of our peti·tion turns. If we fail to get an answer to our prayer, it may be that we do not feel as we ought toward some one. Suppose now you pray for the Lord to bless you, to forgive and guide you, and at the same time you know that there is one individual you hold hardness against, do you think the Good Spirit is coming to bring an answer to your petition? No, it will not; every time you pray with hardness in your heart, according to this model prayer of our Saviour, you virtually say, " Lord, there is one person I hate, I cannot forgive him. I pray thee to forgive me *as* I forgive him." Some people ought to be thankful that their prayers are not answered, for if they were according to the feeling they manifest toward others. I am thinking that

God's curse would come down on them with all its withering power.

It is dangerous business to address the Deity with feelings of hatred or animosity in our hearts toward others. The rule of prayer, which we have presented to us in the prayer of our Saviour, is an excellent one. It brings all classes on to the same level. None can have predominance of others in this respect. The spirit of it must be felt and experienced by all who would seek mercy at the hands of a righteous God. None can come to him in a self-confident, self-righteous manner and meet his approval. All must be penitent, broken-hearted, willing to forgive others, who would secure the divine mercy and blessing. How strange and inconsistent it looks to see two persons in the same meeting, praying to the same God, who do not even *speak to each other.* Can such prayers be heard? Never! Brother, Sister, you must get right. Confess! Forsake!

How strange and inconsistent it looks
again to see those who have once *said,*
they forgave all, talking about and slandering the very person they had forgiven.
Is this the right kind of forgiveness?
Does this kind come from the *heart* or
only from the *lips?* Judge for yourself.
When the Lord forgives He never men-
tions the sin afterwards. He never
brings up any of the old past sins to
throw in the forgiven ones face. Their
sins and iniquities will I *remember no
more.* O what rivers of joy and salvation might flow, if everybody acted on
this principle! What streams of love
and happiness would gladden the pathway of many a sorrowful one, if others
would forgive, and forget their follies!
What power there would be in the
Church, if there were no hardness, no
strifes or divisions. Where is the love
and tenderness of heart that should char-
acterize the followers of Jesus? O, that
the melting power of the Holy Spirit
may come down to soften hard hearts,

to subdue stubborn wills, to uproot pre-
judices, and to produce a forgiving spirit
in those who profess to be followers of
Him who from the Cross of Calvary,
prayed for his enemies saying, " Father,
forgive them, they know not what they
do."

THE GREAT DAY.

REV. VI. 17.

The great day of his wrath is come, and who shall
be able to stand.

The great judgment day. What a
solemn theme to contemplate! Do we
think of it as seriously as we ought? It
is certainly coming. Who can tell how
soon? Suddenly it may burst upon a
guilty world. It is near, it is near, and
hasteth greatly. When God's appointed
hour rolls round, it will come. No human power can stay the onward march
of that tremendous event. Come it will,
come it must. Whether we are dead or
alive, prepared, or unprepared, meet it
we certainly shall. It is the appointed
time for the judgment of the whole
world. That day has been long foretold.
Enoch, the seventh from Adam, prophesied of it. " Behold, the Lord cometh
with ten thousand of his saints, to exe-

cute judgment upon all, and to convince
all, that are ungodly among them, of all
their ungodly deeds which they have
committed, and of all their hard speeches
which ungodly sinners have spoken
against him." Jude 14. 15. He cometh.
Yes Jesus is the appointed Judge. Once
he came to this earth as an innocent
babe. He was poor and despised. The
barn afforded him a shelter, and the
manger a cradle. All his life was one
of poverty and suffering. He was despised and rejected of men, a man of sorrows and acquainted with grief. His
life closed amid the shameful bloody
scenes of Calvary.

But behold him now, coming in the
clouds of heaven. See the dazzling splendor of his regal train. What glory sur-
rounds him. What power attends him.
He is the judge of all mankind. What
a magnificent spectacle. Thousands of
angels await his command. Compared
with this all the glory of earth is but
the faint glimmering of the glowworm

when compared with the dazzling effulgence of the noonday Sun. See! Yonder the heavens depart and the great white throne appears. See the glory flash from him who sits upon it. Who is this! It is the babe of Bethlehem, coming now as King of kings, and Lord of lords. He speaks. The dead hear his voice and come forth. From land and sea they come. What a scene ensues. Let an inspired penman describe it. " And I saw a great white throne and him that sat on it, from whose face the earth and the heaven fled away ; and there was found no place for them. And I saw the dead, small and great, stand before God, and the books were opened ; and another book was opened, which is the book of life; and the dead were judged out of those things which were written in the books, according to their works. And the sea gave up the dead which were in it ; and death and hell (or the grave) delivered up the dead which were in them; and they were judged every man according to their works. And death and hell were cast into the lake of fire. This is the second death. And whosoever was not found written in the book of life was cast into the lake of fire." Rev. 20. 11–15. What an awful day that will be! Is it any wonder that the wicked would like to escape it. A woman once said after a minister had been preaching about the judgment, "O, you frighten me; I hope I shall be in my grave when that day comes." Poor woman! she thought the grave would be a hiding place but she was mistaken. Some tell us the wicked dead will not rise at all, they too are mistaken. The grave will be no hiding place. I read from the words of him who cannot lie that " the hour is coming in the which, all that are in the graves shall hear his voice, and come forth. They that have done good, unto the resurrection of life ; and they that have done evil, unto the resurrection of condemnation." John 5. 28, 29. Again Paul says, " there shall be a resurrection of the dead, both of the just and the unjust." Acts 24. 15. So it will be. Old earth and ocean will be stirred to their very centre, and every particle of mortal dust will come forth. There will be no hiding from the presence of the Judge, no evading his searching investigation. All who have committed suicide, all who have been murdered, all who have been burned to death, all who have been devoured by wild beasts, all who have been eaten by cannibals, all who have been swallowed by earthquakes, and, in a word, all that have ever lived will appear at the judgment. All who ever had an identity here will have an identity there. None can escape. The earth shall cast out her dead. In solemn procession the countless multitudes of earth shall march to the judgment throne to receive their final sentence. Solomon saw this day, and uttered a warning to the young: "Rejoice, O young man, in thy youth; and let thy heart cheer thee in the days of thy youth, and walk in the ways of thine heart, and in the sight of thine eyes: but know thou, that for all these things God will bring thee into judgment." Eccl. 11. 9. If you will sin do it with your eyes open. If you will walk in your own way and gratify your sinful desires do it in the light that flashes from the great white throne. "Know thou that God will bring thee into judgment." Again. "Let us hear the conclusion of the whole matter: Fear God, and keep his commandments: for this is the whole duty of man. For God shall bring every work into judgment, with every secret thing, whether it be good or whether it be evil." Eccl. 12. 13, 14. Seeing then that all shall be there, what a mighty motive this is to repentance. The great question for us to settle is, *how will it be with us?* How will it be with *me?* How will it be with *you?* Shall we be among the saved or lost? Some men's sins are open beforehand, going before to judgment, and some they follow after. Have we confessed our sins and had them all forgiven through faith in the blood of Christ? or are they still lurking about our conscience, causing us to have a fearful looking for of judgment, and fiery indignation which shall devour the adversaries? Salvation or destruction will be our portion. Which? One or the other is inevitable. There is no middle ground. We are either the Lord's or we are the devil's. No man can serve two masters. We are serving one or the other. Even now, this very moment we are on one side or the other. Whose are we? Where are we going? If we were to judge from appearances we should infer that a great many who profess to be following Christ were following the other master. Many are full of pride and vain glory. Did they realize the awful solemnity of that grand and rapidly approaching day, would they not humble themselves before God? What use then for all those ornaments, gewgaws, and adornings, which are but the outward manifestations of inward pride? What use then for idle talk, jesting, joking and evil speaking? What use then for thousands of silver and gold hoarded up, when it ought to have been used in doing good? Can money save us? What use then for a form of godliness without the power? What use then for anything but pure and undefiled religion before God the Father? That will be a searching day. Who shall be able to stand? Are we ready? Is all on the altar? Do we love God with all the heart? Have we any hardness against any one on earth? Do we speak evil of any one? Are we free from condemnation? Has the blood of Jesus cleansed us from all sin? None but the pure in heart shall see God. If we are the Lord's all is right. We can rejoice amid the wreck of matter, and the crash of worlds. The Judge will be be our best Friend. He is our Elder Brother. For us he has purchased the crown of glory, and prepared the mansions of eternal delight. To those on his right hand he will say, "Come ye blessed of my Father, inherit the kingdom prepared for you from the foundation of the world." Beyond the dark clouds of divine wrath, the perdition of the ungodly, and the dissolution of temporal things, rises to view the bright and sunny landscapes of paradise restored: "a new heaven and a new earth wherein dwelleth righteousness." O reader where will you be in that day? Can you bear the thought of being forever lost? You may wear a crown of glory, and bear a palm of eternal victory. Jesus loves you. He died to save you. Will you accept him now? Repent, Pray, Believe. O delay no longer. Haste, haste. Prepare for eternity.

22*

TENDERNESS.

" Be ye kind one to another, tender hearted, forgiving one another, even as God for Christ's sake, hath forgiven you."

It seems to me that there is no point upon which Christians should be more guarded than the one which heads this article. Each and all should endeavor to cultivate a spirit of tenderness and compassion one toward another. I have traveled quite extensively in several states; have attended camp meetings, conferences, and have preached in the country, in villages, in towns and cities ; have visited from house to house, and talked and prayed with the people; but as far as my observation and experience extend I see no point where many professed Christians are deficient so much as in this.

There is a lack of that kindness, and

tenderness of heart, which the apostle here recommends. We have evidently come down to that period in the history of our world, where we may look for the development of those traits of character described by the apostle in his letter to Timothy.

Men were to be lovers of their own selves, covetous, boasters, proud, blasphemers, disobedient to parents, unthankful, unholy, without natural affection, truce breakers, false accusers, incontinent, fierce, despisers of those that are good, traitors, heady, high-minded, lovers of pleasure more than lovers of God; having a form of godliness, but denying the power thereof.

This spirit prevails and increases everywhere. It is not only seen in the unbelieving world, but it abounds just where the inspired writer said it would, among those "having a form of godliness, but denying the power thereof." Now, what is the power of godliness? Is it not love? Does not the church wield the mightiest influence for good when its members love one another? Did not the Savior say, " by this shall all the world know that ye are my disciples, when ye have love one for another?" Where shall the religion of Christ be exhibited if not among his followers? It would seem that the devil has come down with great power, knowing that his time is short; and he is constantly engaged in stirring up envy, malice, hatred, suspicion, jealousies, strife, and evil surmisings among the people of God.

 I know of quite a number of churches that have been torn and mangled in a shocking manner, just because some of their members were willful stubborn, and full of hatred.

Instead of being kind one to another tender-hearted, forgiving one another, when some little offense has arisen, the devil has taken advantage of human nature, and stirred up hard feelings, and created contentions and divisions, until the whole neighborhood

is in an uproar; the lambs are killed,
Christ dishonored; the spirit grieved,
and the way of truth evil spoken of.

My brethren these things ought not
so to be. They need not be. There is a
better way. Let each individual get his
own heart right, and then walk by the
law of kindness. O how many families
and churches might share the hundred
fold of joy and happiness, if all possessed
a tender heart, and were willing to
forgive. How many erring ones might
be reclaimed and brought into the fold
of Christ if tender hearts and kind words
attended their wayward course. Is it
not time there was a change? Ought we
not to open our eyes and see what manner of spirit we are of? Have we been
disputing and contending about doctrines and prophecies until the good
spirit has left us? Have we forgotten
to pray and live near to Jesus? Can
we be followers of the Lamb and not
have his spirit? What saith the Apostle, "Now, if any man have not the

Spirit of Christ he is none of his." If we have the spirit of Jesus, will it make us ugly and full of bitterness and strife? No, no, no. The spirit of our master is a tender spirit. Whoever drinks at this fountain will be a new creature; old things will have passed away. A fountain cannot send forth sweet water and bitter at the same time. If the spirit is in us, like a well of water springing up, our influence will be felt for good upon those around us. The Christian lives and walks with a well of gentleness, goodness and love in his heart. His words and actions have in them a tenderness and fervency that moves upon the hearts of others. Let us, then get nearer to the living fountain. Let us partake more largely of the Spirit of Jesus, who was meek and lowly in heart.

What instructions would Paul give if he were here? Listen to him.—

"Let no corrupt communication proceed out of your mouth, but that which is good to the use of edifying, that it may minister grace unto the hearers. And grieve not the holy spirit of God, whereby ye are sealed unto the day of redemption. Let all bitterness, and wrath and anger, and clamour, and evil speaking, be put away from you with all malice: and be ye kind one to another, tender-hearted, forgiving one another, even as God for Christ's sake hath forgiven you." O how great has been God's love to us! Who can measure it? It is an abyss over which angels bow in deep meditation without fathoming its depths. It is a height to which the wing of brightest cherubim never yet soared. It is a breadth which human imagination never yet embraced. It is a boundless ocean. We are nothing but sinners, enemies; yet God so loved us, that he gave Jesus to suffer and die that we might have eternal life. Our sins have been like scarlet, but, for the sake of his Son he freely forgives us all. His love has followed us all our days. He has forgiven us ten thousand times. His love protects us amid the dangers of the wilderness. His love holds up before us the crown of unfading joys; and his love will bring the faithful safely home to share the raptures and enjoy the endless delights of the paradise of God. O then, in view of the compassion, love and tenderness of our heavenly Father towards us, ought we not to show pity and kindness toward one another? There are sorrowful hearts all around us. One kind word, or gentle look, will send a gleam of sunlight along their gloomy way. Let us forgive as we hope to be forgiven. Let us seek the wandering and the lost, and when the sorrows and conflicts of this life are past, we will sing with the white-robed band on the banks of the river of life.

> " Could we but see what hidden lies,
>   Beneath the outward form ;
> Could we but hear the deep-felt sighs,
>   Which from the heart are drawn.

Or did we see what sorrows hang,
  Like a dark curtain round,
The heart that late so sweetly sang,
  With such a cheerful sound.

Or knew we what the motives are,
  Which govern every deed ;
Or the various things that mar,
  The winding path we lead.

Or did we know the secret wish,
  The effort to do right,
And the temptation they resist,
  Unknown to others sight.

Knew we the *whole* of every mind,
  And *all* that dwells within,
O could we ever be unkind,
  Or cause a soul to sin ?

But would we not more earnest be,
  To cheer the lonely one,
And ever striveto do and speak
  That which would trouble none ? "

23

HINTS FOR HEALTH.

This is for your health.

In erecting a building the *foundation* is usually the first thing to be considered. If this is laid firm, and solid, then the framework and covering may be safely put on; but if the foundation is weak, or rotten, no matter how beautiful the building may appear without, it is unsafe, and in constant danger of falling down. Health is the foundation on which a life of usefulness and happiness must be erected. It should receive the first attention of every individual. Our world is burdened with sick folks. There are probably two-thirds more sick people than there need to be. Why is it? There are some it is true, who are born with weak, sickly constitutions and are never

well from infancy. Such are to be pitied,
for if there is anything pitiful to look
at, it is to see individuals going about
with poor sickly, rickety bodies, not
able to help themselves nor do anything
to help anybody else. But the vast majority of those who are sick have become
so I believe through *ignorance* or *inat-
tention* to *the laws of health.* Man is
under law, physical as well as moral, and
the transgression of law must always be
attended with disastrous consequences.
No man can sin against God or himself
with impunity. We reap what we sow,
whether in a moral or physical sense.
All through the land are thousands suffering to-day, with lingering, painful diseases, just because they have violated
law. Some have done it ignorantly,
some presumptuously, and after the
health has once become impaired it is
hard work to restore it again. It is
much easier to slide down hill, than it
is to climb up. A great responsibility
rests upon parents, or those who have

the care and training of children. At
the cradle is the place to begin. It is
much easier to impress right thoughts,
and inculcate right principles in iufant
minds, than it is to eradicate erroneous
ones from strong minds in after years.
Direct the stream right at its source and
it will run in the right channel. Fasten
the little crooked sprout to a straight
stick or post, and it will grow up a
straight tree; but neglect it, and it will
always be warped, and crooked. Children should be taught right habits in
regard to health. How do they know
what is good for them unless some one
else tells them? If they are allowed to
have their own way, to eat, and drink,
whatever and whenever they have a
mind to, they will grow up with these
ideas. There should be system, order,
regularity in all the domestic arrangements. In order to this, parents should
inform themselves in regard to the laws
of health, that they may be able to im-
part instruction to their children. We

cannot *teach* what we do not know ourselves, and it is certain we cannot *know* much unless we *study.* We possess an intellect, and that intellect should be so well informed as to give right directions to the habits of the body, and the body should be so well governed as to give clearness and power to the intellect. One in a large degree is dependent on the other. A sound mind and a sound body go together. But, if we do not know how to take care of ourselves, how can we give direction to others? Thousands of doctors' bills are paid that no need to be paid. Every person can be his own physician if he will. Doctors' drugs as a general thing, kill more than they cure. Study yourself. Use your own judgment. The world is full of good books, get them, and inform your own mind. If you are sick consult some physician who will not poison you to death with drugs. If you are well have common sense enough not to get sick. Let us look at a few thoughts.

1st. WHAT DO YOU EAT? The stomach is the regulator of the whole physical structure. It is the spring of life and action to the entire body. Derange the digestive organs and you derange the whole system. Some kinds of food are healthy, and some are not; some easy to digest, and some indigestible. Is it not surprising what abominable messes some fond mothers will put into their little children's stomach's? They stuff them until they are sick, and then dose them with doctor's drugs until they die. Some grown up people too will eat all kinds of trash, at all times a day, and then wonder that they " feel bad at the pit of their stomach." Now *reason* would dictate that the stomach should not be overloaded—nothing should be put into it that is indigestible; plain coarse food is the best, and nothing hearty should be eaten just before retiring at night. Some of the healthiest, and hardest working people with whom I am acquainted, eat only twice a day. One rule might not work in all cases; each should study for themselves, and be careful what goes into their stomachs. This is for your health.

2d. *What do you drink?* This question is quite as important as what do you eat. It is claimed by some of the best physicians that hot tea and coffee are very injurious to health. What swill tubs some people make of their stomachs. Swash, swash, goes the tea and coffee, three or four hot cupfuls, three or four times a day. Little children sit down to the table with a hot cup of tea steaming at their plate. So it goes on from year to year. By and by sick headache comes, dyspepsia comes, nervousness comes, and a troop of other annoying diseases come.

"What shall we drink?" say you. Drink something that is *fit* to drink. What did the Lord make the good pure water for? Why are there ten thousand springs of pure, living water all around us? Why the refreshing showers, the

gushing fountains, the sparkling cas-
cades? To give man something to drink.
Why then pour such a mess of liquid
into your stomach as would make a dog
sick if he drank it? Nothing either too
hot or too cold, should go into the stomach It is better not to drink anything
at meal time, and not too large quantities
at any one time. Be temperate both in
eating and drinking. Too much cold
water should not be taken into the stomach when in a state of perspiration.
Wisdom is profitable to direct. Consider this matter well. This is for your
health.

3d. *How often do you bathe?* The body
should be kept clean. There are thousands of little pores on the skin of every
person, that should be kept open,
that the refuse matter may escape from
the system. Some people go from one
year to another, and never wash, except
their hands and face, and some hardly
do that. Is it any wonder that they are
sick? It is sometimes said that, "clean-

liness is next to godliness," and though this is not exactly scripture, yet, it does seem to me, that those who have had their "hearts sprinkled from an evil conscience," will also want their "bodies washed with pure water." We read of "filthy dreamers," and I think the apostle must have had reference to that class who never wash themselves, for if the body is clogged up with filth and dirt, it is no strange thing if the mind is also beclouded with filthy dreams. Come friend, if you are sick go and wash in Jordan, or some other stream seven times, and you will be quite likely to get healed up. Be careful in this matter. Do not bathe in a cold room, nor in water too cold or too warm. Study this subject well. This is for your health.

4th. *How early do you rise in the morning?* I suppose you retire in good season. This is a very important consideration. No man or woman can keep good health a great while who are habitually up late nights. Sleep is nature's great restorer. Nothing will break down a strong constitution faster than to go without sleep. Thousands of young men and women are mere wrecks today, dying with consumption, just because they were out late nights. Think of this. One hour's sleep before midnight is worth two afterward. In order to be out early in the morning it is necessary that you retire in good season. Early rising conduces to health. Then I hope you have your room well-ventilated. Some people sleep from year to year on a filthy old feather bed, and seldom ever open their bedroom windows. It is no wonder that they feel like lounging in bed in the morning, when their system is completely stupefied with bad air. The sleeping apartment shonld be the best room in the house. How refreshing after a good night's rest to rise early and inhale the sweet morning breezes. It gives one new life, new inspiration. The oldest and healthiest people have been early risers. Up and out. Be alive and awake. Search into this matter. This is for your health.

5th. *How much do you exercise in the open air?* Machinery not used gets rusty. Still waters are impure and stagnant. Exercise is essential to health. Sit still and do nothing and you will soon be sick. Run, play, jump, work. Get the pure air of heaven. Fill your lungs. Bathe in the golden sunbeams that make glad the face of nature. Lazy people, and those who are much in-doors are usually peevish and sickly. Those who work much out doors are robust, vigorous and healthy. Boys who live in the country are usually flush with health, because they live plain, keep clean, sleep soundly, work in the sunshine, and exercise freely in the open air. Think of this well. The Lord wants us to have a sound body as well as a sound mind. Control your passions, your temper, and your appetite. This is for your health.

ARE YOU MARRIED?

Eph. v. 33.

"Let every one of you, in particular, so love his wife even as himself; and the wife see that she reverence her husband."

Marriage is one of the most ancient and honorable institutions in the world. It was ordained of God in the garden of Eden and designed to complete the social happiness of man. "And the Lord said it is not good that man should be alone; I will make an help-meet for him. So, causing a deep sleep to fall upon Adam, the Lord took one of his ribs, and closed up the flesh instead thereof; and the rib which he took from man, made he a woman, and brought her unto the man. Then Adam said, This is now bone of my bones, and flesh of my flesh; she shall be called woman because she was taken out of man. Therefore, shall a man leave his father and his mother, and shall cleave unto his wife; and they shall be one flesh." This institution was sanctioned by the Lord Jesus Christ, who manifested his power, in the performance of a noted miracle at a "marriage in Cana of Galilee." The apostle Paul also declares "marriage to be honorable in all." It has its foundation in true and genuine affection, and no parties are prepared to enter into this relation until their hearts are truly united. This condition should not be entered upon lightly or inconsiderately, but reverently, discreetly, and in the fear of God. It is one of the most important steps in life, for in it may be treasured up the happiness or misery of a life-time. Those who take upon themselves the solemn marriage vows should remember that they are not only bound by the law of the land, but by the law of God, to "love, honor and cherish each other until separated by death." What a covenant to enter into—a covenant for life!

How important then, that that which cannot be done but once, be done *right*. Surely, here the divine blessing and guidance should be sought. What spot on earth so lovely as the *home*, where hearts united, seek each others happiness and love, and peace shed continual sunshine. Home is a sweet word, and as new homes are continually being formed how important that those forming them, be rightly instructed, that they may experience all the happiness anticipated. The homes which border nearest on heaven, are those where true love abides, and the will of God is daily performed. It matters not whether it be in a mansion or a cottage. Happiness arises not from outward circumstances, but from the condition of the heart. Love is the basis of all true happiness.

If marriage then is highly conducive to religious and social enjoyment, why is it so often a source of evil? Why are there so many unhappy homes? *Because it is often contracted in opposi-*

tion to the will of God. Believers choose unbelieving companions. The children of God marry with the children of the devil. Christ and Belial are brought together. Is it surprising that those individuals, who trample on the will of God in their marriages, lose his favor or make bitter work for repentance until the end of their lives ?

Consider the following examples which will illustrate the difference between a right and awrong course. "Louise was a beautiful example of female piety. Educated, refined, yet deeply devoted to her Saviour, she adorned her profession with a lustre rarely excelled. Her fellow disciples loved her tenderly. The poor saw her, and were glad for Louise was benevolent. Seldom has the light of piety shone with such brilliancy and purity as it did in the life and actions of this meek, excellent young lady. Never did young Christian give brighter promise of being faithful unto death. Louise was addressed by a young man of excellent moral character, but without piety. A better and more suitable companion in every other respect could not be desired. He was a counterpart to the amiable youth of whom Jesus said—"*One thing thou lackest.*" He sought Louise's hand in marriage. The faith of Louise was sorely tried by this proposal. To reject it was to refuse a most advantageous offer. Beside this she felt a strong attachment toward him. Both interest and affection pleaded, "What shall I do?" He is friendly to religion. He is all that could be desired in a bosom companion, only he is not a Christian. Thus thought Louise. Still in her better judgment, she felt convinced that his being unrenewed ought to be an insuperable barrier to their union. But inclination triumphed, Louise stood at the altar, and plighted the irrevocable vow. Was she happy? Alas! already had she been conscious of spiritual declension. Her intercourse, with her affianced husband, prior to her marriage, had damped the fervor of her zeal. The silent convictions of the conscience that she was wrong had weakened her confidence in God. The wedding day cast a further gloom over her spirit. Its festivities were unsanctified by prayer. The bridegroom's spirit—the spirit of the world—reigned lord of the ascendent. They took possession of their new home, but no family altar was erected there—no secret place was consecrated to closet devotion. The bride and the bridegroom were there, but Christ the bride's master was excluded; or was there only as a secluded guest. At first the husband of Louise attended the house of God with punctuality; he showed no opposition to the great subject of religion. His wife, ventured one day to plead the cause of Christ with him. Then the carnal mind was aroused. He spoke warmly. Henceforth the topic of personal piety is to be interdicted. He would not listen to the name of Louise's master. Very soon he grew weary of going to the house of God. If his wife mentioned to go and leave him at home, he charged her with unkindness, and even threatened to seek amusement from home. Fearful of the results Louise abandoned her seat at Church. The next step of the unconverted husband was to urge his wife to visit social parties, concerts, and other places of amusement. At first she resisted, but by degrees yielded. The church was obliged to cut her off as an unworthy member, and none, who now know the gay and fashionable wife would suspect that she was once the meek, zealous, and devoted lover of Jesus.

Lucy, who belonged to the same church, was not so brilliant a light in the first months of her Christian profession as Louise; but she was truly devoted. Her character was developed by degrees. Every week brought to light excellences unobserved before. Her piety, as the light of the Gospel shone more clearly upon her yielding and submissive heart. Lucy had a suitor of similar attractions and claims to him who became the husband of Louise. A slight intimacy had existed between them prior to her conversion. When she gave up her sins she also gave up her suitor. With a firmness worthy of imitation, she said to him—"I am now a follower of Christ. You walk in an opposite path. We cannot be happy together. When you become a Christian, if desirable, our intercourse can be renewed." The young man, however, showed no inclination for Christian duties. He plunged deeply into the pleasures of sin, married a gay woman and died unconverted. The thoughtless and trifling blamed Lucy for losing so fine an opportunity for a comfortable settlement in life; some of her fellow-disciples, too, joined in their sentence of condemnation; but Lucy felt the satisfaction of one who makes a sacrifice for Christ's sake. She had her reward. A man of acknowledged piety saw her worth and married her. Happiness and piety crowned their union. They walked together in unity of spirit, mutual helpers in the way to Mount Zion. Louise and Lucy are examples of two classes, many of whom I have seen during my ministry; They represent not merely two individuals, but two very large classes; the first of which, it is to be regretted, is constantly increasing in the church of Christ. With their history before him to which class will the young convert decide to belong? Admitting the certainty of similar consequences in almost every case, will you dear reader choose the destiny of Louise? Will you, for the sake of a husband or wife, deliberately forsake your Saviour? Better far to remain unmarried through life than to marry an impenitent sinner, who will lead you from the cross of Christ, and then after embittering your domestic life take you with him to *everlasting perditian.* Look seriously, young Christian at this question. Strip it of that romantic aspect, with which the young mind delights to cover it. The utterance of that irrevocable vow is the most mighty act in life. It forges a bond which no hand but Death's can break. Think seriously? Will you bind your destiny to that of an impenitent sinner? *You*, a follower of the Lord Jesus Christ, wed one, who is following Satan! Is it possible? How can you expect to gain the kingdom in such company? Is eternal life so lightly valued, that you are willing to risk its enjoyment for the sake of the companionship of an ungodly person? Do you love Christ so little, that you are prepared to prefer the love of a dying fellow creature to His friendship? O dreadful preference! Shameful dishonor done to the Lord of glory! Can you dare to hope that if you became thus guilty He will acknowledge you when He comes in His glory with all the holy angels?

Two mariners are in the same port.

Both of them are in command of a noble ship. They are both about to sail on a long and distant voyage.

From the port there are two channels leading to the ocean. One is deep, wide, pleasant and safe. Rarely has a ship experienced any difficulty in sailing there. The other passage is narrow, shallow, abounding in rocks and sand bars. It is so dangerous that scarcely a vessel has ever passed it in safety. It is marked with wrecks, along its entire length. One of these mariners wisely chooses the safe channel, and his ship, with her white sails filled with a favoring breeze, gaily floats out to sea in safety. The other, in opposition to the warning voice of his friends, in defiance of the almost impassable barriers, attempts the shallow passage. He is soon embarrassed by its irregularities. He has to tack from side to side, makes slow progress; every moment his difficulties increase. He attempts to return, but the channel is too narrow to permit this. Soon he runs upon a shoal. Night comes on, the winds rise ; the sea roars; the waves grow tumultuous. In vain he utters useless regrets, and groans forth his foolish sorrows. The angry elements heed not his cries. They know no pity. When the sun rises the mariner is no more! His noble ship has gone to pieces upon the rocks. All is lost, through the folly that would not be warned by the voice of experience. Such is the folly of that young Christian, who willfully disregarding the voices of the past, and the living facts within his own sphere of observation, rushes to the hymeneal altar with a Christless bride or bridegroom.

But what says the Bible in regard to this matter? To this we *must* submit, or totally abandon all hopes of eternal life. " *Can two walk together except they be agreed?*" This is the Lord's question. It commends itself to our common sense, even in the case of ordinary companionship. Agreement in spirit and character is necessary to a common friendship. How much more in the strict intimacy of the marriage bond? How can the carnal mind and the mind of Christ mingle? Such opposite principles brought into fellowship can but produce perpetual differences. Do you choose a marriage with such an inevitable issue? Or do you intend to sell your religious principles for the poor compensation of a God accursed union? To the Jewish church God said: "*Neither shalt thou make marriages with them.*" This prohibition, you see, is peremptory. True, it related to intermarriage with *heathen* families. But where is the difference between the sinner of the Christian community, and the heathen in the Jewish neighborhood? In respect to knowledge the difference is great. But wherein do their hearts differ? God assigned a particular reason, aside from the personal influence of such marriages, for their absolute prohibition. He said, "*They,* (the heathen) *shall turn away thy son from following me.*" Is not this reason applicable to the Christian and the sinner? When in the providence of God, the parties to such unscriptural unions become parents, how sad their influence upon their offspring! What avails it if the religious parent teach the children to pray, to read the holy Bible, to walk in the way of life? Will not the example of the unconverted parent lead them to reply as did a boy who, when his mother rebuked him for swearing, said, "*My father swears.*" What bitter regret, what unavailing sorrow must such a shocking exhibition of parental influence have excited in the foolish woman, who had married such a sinner! Would *you* avoid such an experience? Would *you* escape the misery of an ungodly family? Then, marry not with an unconverted man or woman. Be fixed on this point. Live and die unmarried, or marry only a fellow laborer in Christ.

The language of the New Testament is equally positive and unequivocal. "*Be*

*not unequally yoked together with unbe-
lievers,*" wrote Paul to the Corinthian
Church. Of a widow, also, after show·
ing her right to a second marriage, he
said: "*She is at liberty to be married to
whom she will, only in the Lord.*" She
had no right as a Christian woman to
marry out of Christ. No! as a believer,
she could have no part with Belial. She
must marry *only in the Lord.* Is not
this authoritative? Do not these texts
absolutely *forbid* the intermarriage of
believers with unbelievers? To me, it
seems, that language could not make the
prohibition more clear. And that dis·
ciple, who in its face proceeds to the
formation of such a marriage, is guilty
of *willful* sin. Once more, then, I im·
plore you dear young convert, to set
your heart against the idea of marrying
a Christless person. You may have an
opportunity to secure wealth and social
consideration by such a marriage. Spurn
such an idea. True affection must form
the basis of a genuine marriage. Or you

may be lured by the hope of converting your partner to Christ. The hope is only a fond delusion. You will rather be drawn from Christ. Be not deceived. Such conversions rarely occur. Scripture experience, and common sense combine to show that marriages of believers with unbelievers, are fatal to the piety of the former, and by no means beneficial to the latter." Beware of those who have a mere form of godliness. True piety consists in something more than a union with a visible church, and a participation in religious ceremonies. It consists in a thorough change of heart, and a strict conformity of life to the requirements of the gospel. Be not hasty. Seek the will of God, and the companionship of the holy. Time is too short, and life too precious to be thrown away. " Whether, therefore, ye eat, or drink, or whatsoever ye do, do all to the glory of God."

COMFORT IN AFFLICTION.

" When thou passest through the waters, I will be with thee; and through the rivers, they shall not overflow thee; when thou walkest through the fire, thou shalt not be burned; neither shall the flame kindle upon thee."

How comforting are these words! They fall like sweet music on the ear. They lift the heart from the depths of its sadness, and shed a gleam of sunlight into the dark chambers of the afflicted mind. The Lord is good. He will not leave his children to pass through the deep waters of trouble unprotected and unsupported. The flame shall not kindle upon thee; neither shall the floods overflow thee. Through all the history of the past his goodness has been manifested toward his people. His providence has ever guarded and sustained them; His bounty has ever supplied all their wants; His grace has ever been sufficient to save them from the power and effects of sin; His mercy has ever been imparted to forgive their transgres-sions; and His consolations have ever abounded to comfort them in all their tribulations. However dark and peril-ous the condition of his people, his grace has ever been sufficient for them. It is so today. Not one drop of sorrow more than is necessary will be dealt out to His saints. No believer can calculate upon exemption from affliction. Rela-tionship to God, holiness of heart, eleva-tion of the mind above carnality, will not exempt christians from trials; these are necessary to promote spirituality. The most of general rules have excep-tions, but this is ever an exception to all general rules, for it is a general rule without an exception. The Psalmist said, " many are the afflictions of the righteous," and the experience of all saints confirms the truthfulness of his statement. It is through much tribula-

25*

tion that we must enter the kingdom of God. He who led his people of old through the dark and dangerous path-ways of the wilderness, that they might come to the borders of the "goodly land," is still leading those who trust him, through all the perils of their christian pilgrimage, that they may come to the better country, where all tears shall be wiped away. Just beyond the wilderness and the swelling waves of Jordan, there lie the sunlit hills, and the ever verdant plains of Paradise. Our trials here, will only make our rest sweeter there.

" The path of sorrow, and that path alone,
　Leads to the land where sorrow is unknown.
　No traveler e'er reached that blest abode,
　Who found not briers and thorns in his road.
　The world may dance along the flower plain,
　Cheered as they go by many a sprightly strain.
　Where nature has her mossy velvet spread,
　With unshod feet they yet securely tread :
　But he who knew what human hearts would prove,
　How slow to learn the dictates of his love;
　That, hard by nature, and of stubborn will,
　A life of ease would make them harder still;
　In pity to the sinners he designed

To rescue from the ruins of mankind,
Called for a cloud to darken all their years,
And said, ' Go, spend them in the vale of tears.' "

Yes, afflictions come from a Father's hand, and He knows what is good for us. We are so prone to sin, and to wander from the pathway of righteousness, that He sees it necessary to lead us through the dark waters of sorrow, or the fiery trials of disappointment, in order to wean us from earth, and induce us to aspire after heaven. " Whom the Lord loveth he chasteneth, and scourgeth every son whom he receiveth. Now, no chastening for the present seemeth to be joyous, but grievous; nevertheless, afterward it yieldeth the peaceable fruit of righteousness unto them which are exercised thereby. Wherefore lift up the hands which hang down, and the feeble knees; and make straight paths for your feet, lest that which is lame be turned out of the way; but let it rather be healed." O child of affliction, do the hands of your faith hang down, and do the knees of your hope tremble? Are you almost ready to faint by the way? Are the waters deep, and do the fires burn fiercely? Have loved ones been torn from your embrace, and do you weep as you recall the past? Have the floods and flames devoured all your worldly possessions? Do friends persecute you, and has the tongue of slander tarnished your reputation? Has disease shattered your mortal frame, and do you see months of vanity, and are wearisome nights appointed unto you? Is the past dark, and is the future cheerless? Do the floods and flames still roll around you with unabated fury? O despair not, there is comfort for thee. Hear the voice of your heavenly Father. "Fear not: when thou passest through the waters, I will be with thee; and through the rivers they shall not overflow thee; when thou walkest through the fire, thou shalt not be burned; neither shall the flame kindle upon thee." Hear the voice of your loving Saviour. "These things

I have spoken unto you, that in me ye might have peace. In the world ye shall have tribulation: but be of good cheer; I have overcome the world"? Cheer up then, dear afflicted saint there is hope for thee. There is One who cares for thee, and who will stand by thee in all thy afflictions. Only trust Him, and you shall come forth as gold tried in the fire. Even now you may be able to exclaim with the Apostle, "We glory in tribulations also: knowing that tribulation worketh patience; and patience, experience; and experience, hope; and hope maketh not ashamed; because the love of God is shed abroad in our hearts by the Holy Ghost which is given unto us." Even now you may "think it not strange concerning the fiery trial which is to try you, as though some strange thing had happened unto you: but rejoice, inasmuch as ye are partakers of Christ's sufferings; that when His glory shall be revealed, ye may be glad also with exceeding joy."

It is true that Satan and wicked men may have a sinful hand in many of the afflictions of the righteous; but the Lord has a superintending, overruling and gracious hand. Without his permissive hand, they would never take place; without his restraining hand, they would be overwhelming; without his supporting hand, they would be intolerable; and without his sanctifying hand, they would never be blessed. Sweet is the assurance that "all things work together for good to them that love God." The wheat is not ripened by sunshine alone; it must go through with its months of wind, and rain, and storm. The precious seed requires the fan to blow away the chaff. The gold requires the furnace to purge away the dross. The winds of winter show which of the trees are evergreen and which are not. Trials and afflictions are useful in the same way. God tests his people. Fire and water are purifying elements. "It is good for me that I have been afflicted, for before I was afflicted, I went astray." So said David, and may not many others say the same.

"How happy it is for me that the world often gives me the slip, that I may forsake the world and look out more for the better country; that men often prove false to me, that I may rely on the God of truth; that wants beset me on every side, that I by faith may set myself down by the gate of heaven, and, in the promise, and in his fullness, find a rich supply; that death now and then cuts off a relative, that I may more and more remember my own end, the immortal world, and Him who is the resurrection and the life. Afflictions render the creature tasteless, the world barren, and dispels the intoxicating juice of carnal pleasures and sensual delights. It breaks the sleep of security, and awakens and rouses to duty. Even the saints themselves are more frequent in their devotions under the rod of affliction; and many in trouble visit the throne of grace—dear throne! to which all have access—and pour out a prayer, when his chastening hand is upon them, who before were utter strangers both to the place and the employment."

Blessed affliction! How much it has accomplished for human beings. But it will soon be forever ended. Weeping endureth for a night, but joy cometh in the morning. Only a little while and the shadows of Time will be merged in the splendors of Eternity.

NO NIGHT.

REV. XXI. 25.

" There shall be no night there."

" No night of sorrow shall be there,
    All griefs, all sighs are o'er
No bleeding heart, no tear dimmed eyes,
    On that celestial shore;
God, with his gentle hand of love,
    Shall wipe all tears away,
And in his presence we shall joy,
    Secure in cloudless day.

No night of sin can enter there,
    Like Jesus we shall be,
For we shall see him as he is,
    And holy be as he;
No wandering thoughts, no anxious cares
    Shall agitate our breast,
No sin shall mar our services
    In yonder land of rest.

No night of ignorance is there,
    We'll know as we are known,
And through a blest eternity,
    Rejoice before the throne;
No clouds shall e'er o'ershadow us ;
    Faith shall be changed to sight,
All gloomy doubts and fears dispelled,
    In that fair land of light.

No night of suffering is there,
  No weariness, no pain,
The ransomed in that better land
  Shall ne'er be sick again;
No aching head , no fevered brow
  Shall weigh our bodies down,
For in Immanuel's happy land,
  All sickness is unknown.

No night of parting shall be there,
  Our loved are gone before,
We 'll meet them in that better land,
  And meet to part no more;
To be forever with the Lord,
  Our griefs, our trials o'er,
No tearful eye, no sad farewell
  On yonder radiant shore.

No night of death can enter there
  To close our peaceful rest,
No tender ties are severed
  In the mansions of the blest;
Once in our happy longed for home,
  We are safe for evermore,
For ah ! no night can enter
  On that celestial shore."

SALVATION.

2 Tim. ii. 10.

" The salvation which is in Christ Jesus with
eternal glory."

Salvation ! how much that word implies. It has two aspects, when used in
the sense of which I am about to speak—
present and future. I believe that the
saints of God know something of a present salvation. They are saved from
sin. They are justified by faith and
have peace with God, through our Lord
Jesut Christ. Sin does not reign in
them nor rule over them. They have
found a way of deliverance from it.
They *know* that Jesus *has* saved them,
and *does* keep them from sin, because
they trust in Him. For a person to say
that he is a Christian, and at the same
time to say that he is a sinner, seems to
me to be a contradiction of terms.

What ! a Christian and a sinner at the same time? How can this be? A follower of Christ, and living in violation of his will? Is it possible? No, it cannot be so. If you are a Christian then you delight to keep Christ's commandments. It is not boasting to say that we are saved *now*—that we have passed from death unto life—that we have the witness of the spirit. It is giving honor to the Lord Jesus Christ, who has accomplished the work for us. He is a perfect Saviour. He does not forgive a part of our sins when we come to him for pardon. He forgives *all*. He cleanses us from every secret fault, removes every stain and trace of guilt, and makes us *new creatures*. It is impossible to be partly saved, and partly lost, at the same time. There is no middle ground. We are either saints or sinners. We cannot serve two masters. We are one thing or the other. Christ does his work thoroughly. He is no half way Saviour.

He saves his people *from* their sins not
in them.

When He was on earth, He manifested
this power. One came to him who had
been a notorious sinner. She believed
he was the Son of God, and she loved
him, but she felt so sinful and unworthy
that she hardly dared to look him in the
face. So, bowing in his presence, she
wept, and with her flowing locks and
falling tears she washed his feet. Did
Jesus speak harshly or bid her go away?
No. Did he accuse her of the wrong
she had done? No. Did he despise
her because she was despised by others?
No. He could read penitence in those
tears. He knew how deeply sorry she
felt for all her sins, and his great loving
heart was moved with compassion.
He came to seek and to save the lost,
and here was a lost sinner bowed in
penitence at his feet. Could he turn
her away? *Never.* How kindly he addressed her--" Woman, thy sins are forgiven, thy faith hath saved thee; go in

peace." O, how sweetly these words fell upon the heart of that sinner! What joy lit up her countenance! What peace she experienced. She was still a *woman.* Jesus, the son of the highest, listened to *her*, noticed *her*, poor and wretched as she felt, and addressed her as a woman! Yes, "*woman* thy sins are forgiven, thy faith hath saved thee; go in peace." Was she saved? Who dares say she was not? The work was done with just one word from Jesus. She was saved, gloriously saved. All her sins were forgiven and she became a meek follower of Jesus. "O" say you, "this was a great while ago, and the Saviour was here on earth." Yes, but has he any less power to day. Is he less merciful now? Did he not die on the cross for his enemies? Was he not raised again for our justification? Did he not ascend to heaven to give repentance and remission of sins to all that would call upon him? Was he not exalted as a prince and a saviour? Is not his blood still efficacious to cleanse from the foulest sins? Have not thousands been washed in the all-cleansing fountain? Is not the invitation still published, " Whosoever will let him come?" O doubt no longer. Only believe and you shall be saved. Come, just as you are. Jesus loves you. He is looking at you with pity just now. He never yet turned one away who sought him with a penitent heart. If you have started and fallen a hundred times never give up. Try again. He is able to save to the uttermost, all who come to him. His blood cleanseth from *all* sin. Great sins and little sins, private sins and public sins, occasional sins and besetting sins, all sin, yes, his blood " cleanseth from *all* sin." Now? Yes, now, this very moment, if you will let him. He can save you from sin, and he can *keep you from sinning? Do you believe it?*

"There is therefore *now* no condemnation to them which are in Christ Jesus, who walk not after the flesh, but after the Spirit." O follow the leadings of the Spirit. Yield not to the lusts of the flesh. Confess and forsake your sins, and you shall know the joys of God's salvation.

There is a deep and rich experience for every one who will truly follow Jesus in this life. Multitudes of professors know nothing of present salvation—of freedom from sin,—of the cleansing, comforting, and strengthening power of the Holy Spirit—of the peace that passeth understanding—of the joy unspeakable and full of glory. They know not what it is to count all things as loss for Christ, to glory in tribulations, and to go without the camp, bearing reproach for Christ's sake. They think that, if they can have Christ and plenty of money, Christ and plenty of good clothes, Christ and plenty of friends, Christ and a good name, Christ and worldly pleasures, Christ and popularity, it is all very nice. But Christ and poverty, Christ and poor clothes, Christ and per-

secution, Christ and affliction, Christ and
few friends, Christ and no worldly pleasures, Christ and self-denial, is something that they do not care much about.
It is only those, however, who have given
all for Christ, that know what it is to
have Christ *in* them the hope of glory.
We believe there are some who have
made the full consecration, and who
know what present salvation means.
Christ was made perfect through sufferings, that he might become the author
of present and eternal salvation to all
them who *obey* him. Can we expect
to share in the benefits of his death,
or resurrection, or intercession, or glorious reign, while we live in disobedience? Is it any wonder that there are
so many who are destitute of spiritual life and power, when they are living in disobedience to God's commands?
Salvation is *in* Christ, not out of him.
We can only be partakers of it as we
abide in him. He is the author of
it. He purchased it. He gives it. We

can *abide* in him by *faith* and *obedience.* "If ye abide in me, and my words abide in you, ye shall ask what ye will, and it shall be done unto you." Here is the secret of present salvation. It is to abide in Christ. Not in him by profession merely, but in him by a living, vital faith. Ask what ye will and it shall be done unto you. Are you saved? Search closely. Salvation in this world is to be succeeded with eternal glory in the world to come. Having been saved from sin through faith in the Lord Jesus Christ, we shall be saved eternally when he comes the "second time without sin unto salvation." Then we shall know what future salvation means. The grave must give up its dust. He, who rose triumphant from the tomb, and ascended on high with the keys of death, is coming again to unlock every grave and bring his people home. From yonder lovely resting place our loved ones will· come. How joyful it will be to meet them once more!

We have often wept, and our pathway has seemed lonely since they left us, but O we shall greet them again! Mother, you will clasp that little one in your arms again, and know that it is your own sweet babe that you lost so long ago. There, husbands and wives, parents and children, brothers and sisters will meet and never part again. All tears will be wiped away, and the glory of that re-union will be so great, that we shall forget the sorrows of our earthly pilgrimage. There we shall have glorious bodies, glorious associations, a glorious home, glorious crowns, glorious robes, and sing glorious songs. Even now, in anticipation of that glory, we can say with Paul, "Our light affliction which is but for a moment, worketh for us a far more exceeding and eternal weight of glory. While we look not at the things which are seen, but at the things which are not seen. For the things which are seen are temporal, but the things which are not seen are eternal."

We have hope of eternal life. If we die, we shall live again. If we live till our Lord comes we shall be changed, in a moment, in the twinkling of an eye. This mortal will put on immortality, this corruptible incorruption. Salvation, in its completeness, will bring back the earth to more than its primeval loveliness, and fill it with the glory of God. Its desert places shall blossom as the rose, and its wilderness regions be turned into gardens of delight. Instead of the thorn shall come up the fir tree, and instead of the brier shall come up the myrtle tree, and it shall be to the Lord for a name, for an everlasting sign that shall not be cut off. No sin, sorrow, or death there, but purity, joy, and eternal blessedness. Then the ransomed of the Lord shall return, and come to Zion with songs, and everlasting joy upon their heads, they shall obtain joy and gladness, and sorrow and sighing shall flee away. Will you go to that beautiful land? Will you be saved with an everlasting salvation? Jesus is the way. He can save you from *sin now*, and save you from *death hereafter*. Will you *let* Him save you?

> " Sinner go, will you go
> To the highlands of Eden,
> Where the storms never blow
> And the long Summer's given.
> Where the bright blooming flowers
> Are their odors emitting,
> And the leaves of the bowers
> In the breezes are flitting.
>
> Where the saints robed in white
> Cleansed in life's flowing fountain,
> Shining beauteous and bright,
> They inhabit the mountain.
> Where no sin nor dismay,
> Neither trouble nor sorrow,
> Will be felt for to day,
> Nor be feared for to-morrow.
>
> He's prepared thee a home,
> Sinner, can'st thou believe it,
> And invites thee to come—
> Sinner come and receive it.
> O haste sinner, haste,
> For the tide is receding,
> And the Saviour will soon,
> And forever, cease pleading."

27

THE WAY TO BE HAPPY.

JOHN XIII. 17.

If ye know these things, happy are ye if ye do them.

The first step in the road to happiness is to get a *clean* conscience. Make things all right with the Lord.

Multitudes to-day are seeking happiness, but they are seeking it in the wrong way. They never will find it until their hearts are right with God. They have sinned and *they know* it, and God knows it, and however much they may try to *appear* happy they are not *really* happy. There is trouble within. Holiness comes first, then happiness. The wisdom that is from above is first *pure*, then peaceable. This is God's order. He will not bless us in our sins, but he calls upon us to repent and pray, to confess and forsake our sins, and then we shall obtain mercy.

If we regard iniquity in our hearts we had might as well whistle as to pray, for God will not hear us; but when we come to Him in sincerity, then He will listen to our cry and bestow upon us the blessing we need. As long as we carry about within us a guilty conscience, it is impossible to be happy. There may be transient flights of joy, as is sometimes seen among the gay pleasure lovers, but within there is sorrow and unrest. Guilt in the heart spoils the happiness of life. It is like a worm in a tree, constantly eating at the very core of its life, and causing the beauty of its foliage to wither, fade, and die.

Would you be happy, get rid of the poison of sin. Flee to the open fountain of a Saviour's blood. Pray God, for the sake of His Son, to cleanse you from all sin, and give you a pure heart. When this is done a sweet and heavenly peace will fill your soul. No longer tossed

and distressed like the ocean in a storm,
but calm and peaceful as the waveless
current of a steady flowing stream.   No
longer wild and furious as a madman
bound with chains, but gentle and tranquil as an infant sleeping on its mother's
bosom.   The best way to get through
this world is to be constantly taking
everything to God in prayer.   Are you
troubled and perplexed? Do a multitude of cares press upon you? Cast your
burdens on the Lord.   *He* careth for
you.   Let your faith cling to the promise, " I will never leave thee nor forsake
thee."   We should be like the old col-
ored woman, who, when persecuted, only
replied, " I must tell the Lord."   Ah!
this is the secret of a happy life.   Tell
the Lord.   Pray.   Believe.

> " O what peace we often forfeit,
> Oh what needless pain we bear,
> All because we do not carry
> Everything to God in prayer.
> Can we find a friend so faithful,
> Who will all our sorrows share?
> Jesus knows our every weakness,
> Take it to the Lord in prayer."

Try this way and see if you do not find happiness such as you never experienced before. Take the Bible and learn what is required of you, and then ask Jesus to help you keep his commandments. "If ye know these things, happy are ye if ye do them." Try it and see if heavenly light does not break into your mind. Happiness will light up your countenance, as sunlight gild's the mountain tops when the darkness has disappeared. Another way to promote happiness is to *Sing.* Singing is one of God's best and choicest gifts. How dark this world would be if there were no sweet voices to sing. All nature sings. Even now as I write the birds are chirping and singing around the old farm house door. How happy they seem to be. I thank God for the beautiful birds, they teach us how to be happy.

How can a Christian lounge in bed until the sun is three or four hours high, when the sweet little birds are picking

27*

out their notes by the first streaks of
the morning light. Away with this lazy,
gloomy long faced religion. Up and out
ere the sun shines in at thy window,
and the birds cease their morning song.
God's religion makes us happy. He
puts the sing into our hearts and bids
us go on our way rejoicing. Are you
cast down and discouraged ? Do dark
shadows hang over your pathway ? Sing.
Wake up the mirthfulness of your nature. Be cheerful. Singing praises to
God will drive away the devil, and fill
your heart with joy unspeakable. How
happy David was. Hear him. "Be
glad in the Lord, and rejoice, ye righteous; and shout for joy all ye that are
upright in heart. Rejoice in the Lord,
O ye righteous; for praise is comely for
the upright. Sing aloud unto God our
strength ; make a joyful noise unto the
God of Jacob." "O" says one, "I am
no singer. I cannot carry a tune. How
happy I should be if I could sing." Well
if you cannot sing, "make a joyful noise

unto the Lord." Get your mouth open. Give vent to the emotion of your heart. Praise the Lord. Think of his mercies. How beautiful he has made this world. See the sun pouring down its floods of golden light. See the fields and groves clothed with verdure and beauty. Gaze up at the starry heavens, and see the worlds of light flashing and sparkling their Creator's praise. Can we be dumb? Do we not catch the inspiration that gladdens the face of nature? The birds, the streams, the trees, the rocks, the hills, the fields, the stars—everything says "Sing and give thanks." If clouds lower about you blow them away with the breath of song.

When David was overwhelmed with sorrow, he would sing and pray until the darkness fled, and the light of heaven shone around him. The Lord was his light and his salvation. He gave him songs in the night. He brought him up out of the horrible pit and put a new song in his mouth. Paul and Silas with bleeding backs and aching limbs, prayed and sang praises at the midnight hour, until the old prison at Philipi was lit up with celestial brightness. Martyrs have sung in the midst of flames and shouted praises to God, with lips quivering in death. We have visited the hovels of the poor, the sick and the dying, and have found them rejoicing in a Saviour's love. When we think how much others have suffered before us, and how happy they have been in the midst of all their afflictions, can we be fretful or unhappy? Let us rather sing and give thanks, and show by so doing that we are followers of them who through faith and patience inherit the promises. Do you want your children to be happy? then let them sing. Do you want your home circle to be beautiful and lovely as a garden of flowers? then make it cheerful and attractive. Do you want your prayer-meetings to be seasons of joy and refreshing? then sing in the spirit. Do you want your own heart to be a well-spring of happiness, pouring its streams of gladness on all around? then let the word of Christ dwell in you richly in all wisdom, and sing and make melody with grace in your heart to the Lord.

RAYS OF LIGHT.

Psalm cxix. 129, 130.

" Thy testimonies are wonderful: the entrance of
thy words giveth light."

The best book that ever was printed
is the Bible.   There are a vast number
of good books in the world, and it seems
to me that even the poorest families
might obtain a library in these days,
when books can be purchased at such a
small cost.   Books are worth more than
money or fine clothes, and with a little
economy and self-denial in worldly
things, many dollars could be saved with
which to fill up the shelves of the family
library.   Yet books are of but little
value, only as they are studied.   One
volume well studied is of more value
than many volumes not studied at all.
The man of one book is often more in-
telligent than the man of many volumes,

from the fact that he studies his one,
more than the other does his many. But
I took up my pen to say something
about the Bible. This is the book of
books. The truths of this book are of
more value than the knowledge of all
other books combined. Whatever other
volumes we may lack let us not be destitute of this. However ignorant we may
be of other things, let us not be ignorant of the Bible.

" Most wondrous book ! bright candle of the Lord,
  Star of eternity ! the only star
  By which the bark of man can navigate
  The sea of life and gain the coast of bliss
  Securely; only star which rose on Time,
  And on its dark and troubled billows still,
  As generation, drifting swiftly by,
  Succeeded generation, threw a ray
  Of heaven's own light, and to the hills of God—
  The everlasting hills—pointed the sinner's eye."

Is it surprising that the psalmist
should exclaim, " Thy testimonies are
wonderful ! " Surely the Bible is the
most wonderful book that mortal eye
ever gazed upon.

1st. It is wonderful in its *Origin.*— Not by human wisdom or ingenuity did this book come. All the combined wisdom of the universe could not have produced such a volume. It is the production of an infinite mind. He, who created the heavens and the earth—the eternal God—infinite in wisdom and power—has handed down to man a transcript of his holy mind and will. Through the agency of His divine spirit in taking possession of human intellects, he has communicated to us his thoughts. "The prophecy came not in old time, by the will of man: but holy men of God spake as they were moved upon by the Holy Ghost. " All Scripture is given by inspiration of God, and is profitable for doctrine, for reproof, for correction, for instruction in righteousness: That the man of God may be perfect, thoroughly furnished unto all good works."—2 Tim. 3, 16, 17.

2d. It is wonderful in its *Purity.* It is not like some books which present a fair exterior, while within there are thoughts to corrupt the imagination. Everything here is pure. It is a holy book. It came from a pure source, it was written by pure men, and it purifies the hearts of all who believe and practice its teachings. It has elevated society and civilized nations more than all other volumes. Where can such a pure code of morals be found as in this book? What are the sacred books of false worshippers compared with the Christian's Bible? Do idolators teach and practice holiness? Look over the world and mark well, where the Bible is received, and where it is not. Shall we have it in our schools? Shall we have it in our families? Shall we let our children read it? "Wherewithal shall a young man cleanse his way? by taking heed thereto according to thy word." Ps. cxix. 9.

3d. It is wonderful in its *Unity*. It does not contradict itself. It is composed of different books, written by

28

men unknown to each other, who lived
hundreds of years apart, yet they are
all in harmony. It is not an instrument
whose notes do not vibrate together—
its music is harmonious from Genesis to
Revalation. Moses does not disagree
with John, and John does not disagree
with Moses. Paul does not contradict
Isaiah, and Isaiah does not contradict
Paul. The old and New Testament are
in perfect unison. All the sacred wri-
ters agree with each other—all discourse
on the same grand and glorious themes
There may be some apparent discrepan-
cies, which skeptics and infidels may
catch at, but a little study and careful,
honest criticism will make all plain, and
show the Bible to be a wonderfully
harmonious book.

4th. It is wonderful in *Simplicity*.
Its language is plain and easy to be
comprehended. The unlearned can understand it. It does not come to us
clothed in such high flown sentences that
we need to have a doctor of divinity to

explain it. We can read it for ourselves and exercise the same common sense in understanding it, that we would in reading any other book. The men who were chosen to write this book, were men of great wisdom and simplicity is a mark of wisdom. They used language that the common people could understand. The great majority of the human family are unlearned, and were the language of the Bible, not simple and easy to be understood, only few could receive bene-fit from it. But it is. Divine wisdom knew what man needed, and He has provided a book that all can read and understand.

5th. It is wonderful in *Profundity*. Though its language is plain yet there are depths of wisdom which have not been penetrated. This book challenges the mightiest intellects to comprehend its prophecies. Here the deepest reasoners, the profoundest thinkers, the greatest scholars may come and find a match for all their wisdom. Many have gone down into this treasure-house, and brought out things new and old, and still there are depths of knowledge yet to be discovered.

One who possessed a master-intellect, while surveying the wonders of this book, exclaimed. " O, the depth of the riches, both of the wisdom and knowledge of God ! how unsearchable are his judgments and his ways past finding out. For who hath known the mind of the Lord ? or who hath been his counsellor ?" and it is said that even the " angels desire to look into these things."

6th. It is wonderful in *Variety.* Here we may come and find something always interesting. Here is history, and poetry, and chemistry, and botany, and geology, and astronomy, and physiology, and biography, and geography, and geology, and theology. What a variety of subjects for the intellect to feed upon ! Once I visited a Natural History Museum and saw such a collection of natural curiosities as I never saw before. I looked and looked at dif-ent objects gathered from all parts of the world, until my eyes were weary, and I turned away to think of the wonderful things I had seen. The Bible is a *Museum* in which are gathered the treasures of the ages. Here is such a variety of the grand, the an-cient, and the beautiful in Nature, Art and Grace as will interest all class-es. Open the doors of this Temple and walk in, free of charge. Here gather wisdom from the treasure-house of Divine knowledge.

7th. It is wonderful in *Veracity*. It is the word of truth, the gospel of salva-tion. There are many books we may read and for a time take an interest in them, but when we learn that they are fiction, and not fact, we lose our interest. They cease to retain their hold upon our mind. Man likes something that he can rely upon. Here we have it. The Bible is not a cunningly devised fable. It carries within itself the evidence of its truthfulness. No person can read it with an honest mind, without being convinced that it is true. It describes human nature accurately, and not only this, but the fulfilment of its prophecies demonstrates it to be infallible. Every statement here is unfailing. Pilate once asked the question, " What is Truth?" and the Saviour in his last prayer for his disciples furnishes an answer: " Sanctify them through thy truth, thy word is truth."

8th. It is wonderful in its *Freshness.* Other books we get weary of. After having read them through, we lay them one side, and they seem old to us. We care not to read them again. Not so with this volume. Like the returning dews of morning, which seem ever fresh and delightful, so the Bible as often as we read it seems always new. Those very chapters which we committed to memory in childhood, which we repeated in Sabbath School, and which we have read hundreds of times since, seem just as fresh now and more so, as when first our infant lips uttered them. There is an inexpressible sweetness about the Scriptures. "Thy words were found, and I did eat them; and thy word was unto me the joy and rejoicing of mine heart." More to be desired is this word, than gold, yea, than much fine gold, sweeter also than honey and the honey comb.

9th. It is wonderful in its *Adaptation to Human Necessity.* Have you not been surprised in reading the Scriptures, to find how perfectly adapted they were to your necessities. You felt a hungering and thirsting after something to feed your spiritual nature upon, and here you found it. It gave you light, and comfort and strength as no other book could. It is by partaking of the sincere milk of the word that converts grow, and become strong. Man cannot live by bread alone, but by every word that proceedeth out of the mouth of God.

Here is something that will meet the necessities of all classes, and conditions of men. . Here the young may find instruction, the aged a staff to lean upon, the perplexed a light to guide them, the sorrowful a hope to cheer them, the dying a friend that will stand by them. Here is something adapted to every phase of human experience.

10th. It is wonderful in its *Power*. No words have swept on with such power through the ages as this Word. It is quick and powerful, and sharper than a two edged sword. Skepticism, infidelity, superstition, idolatry and spiritualism cannot stand before the power of Divine Truth. It searches, pierces, and discovers the thoughts and intents of the heart. It is a light that makes bare the darkness of iniquity. Every opposing element that comes dashing against this Rock will spend its force in vain. What wonderful victories have been achieved through the Bible. It has been the power of God unto salvation to countless believing hearts. Still it sweeps on and triumphs. Clear the track when you see this train coming, for it is the train of God's eternal truth, and heaven and earth will sooner pass away, than one jot or tittle of this word fail to be fulfilled.

11th. It is wonderful in its *Preservation*. The time has been when its enemies sought to destroy it. They hunted and searched, and every Bible that could be found was destroyed. Yet, the blessed Book lived. In the dark ages, when persecution raged, when Roman Catholicism prevailed, when Protestants were martyred by millions, when it seemed as if the light of the Gospel would be entirely extinguished, even then, the word of God lived, and came forth in the great Reformation, to shed its light far and wide over the nations. How wonderful the Bible has been in its circulation within the last century. Millions and millions of Bibles have been published and sent into every land.

None need be without a copy of the Holy Scriptures now, for if any are too poor to buy, they can have one free of cost. Missionaries are ready to carry a Bible to every door where it is needed. In this we rejoice, not only because the poor have the gospel preached to them, but because the prophecies are being fulfilled which indicate the dawning of a bright and better day. Never shall I forget the first copy of the Bible that I ever called my own. Let me tell you how it was. Not many years ago I was a small lad living on a farm in the country. A minister moved into our neighborhood and began to hold meetings in the farm houses, from week to week. With other young friends I attended them and listened to the preaching, but was ignorant and somewhat careless of religious things. Soon the Spirit strove with me. I saw myself a sinner and realized my need of a Saviour. One evening after the minister had finished his sermon, I arose and made known my feelings, and asked an interest in the prayers of Christians. They prayed earnestly for me, and I began to pray for myself. It was not long before light broke into my mind, and I felt that I was forgiven. The dark cloud that had hovered over my path for a number of weeks was now banished. All nature seemed to praise God, and I was really a happy convert. Truly I could sing—

> " Jesus all the day long
> Is my joy and my song;
> O that more his salvation I might see;
> Thou hast loved me, I cried,
> Thou hast suffered and died,
> To redeem such a rebel as me."

But I had no Bible, no guide book, no lamp to my path. I was ignorant of what to do or how to live a Christian. I thirsted for more light, for more instruction. Some how or other I obtained fifty cents and away I hastened to the nearest store, and bought my first copy of the precious Bible. It was a cheap one, fine print, with no references between the verses, or on the margin ; but I thought it was the sweetest and prettiest book that I had ever seen. I began at Genesis and read it through. It was my companion by night and day. When I arose in the morning, I read it; when I returned from the field at noon and at night, I read it; when I went to meeting I took it with me. My little Bible was my daily companion. I thought more of it, no doubt, than some men think of thousands of dollars. And did I prize it too highly? No. When I spent that fifty cents for a Bible it was the best bargain I ever made. It was the beginning of a new life to me. That money was deposited in Heaven's bank and will draw interest to all eternity. Two years from that time, at the age of seventeen, I began to preach the Gospel. Since then, I have attended thousands of religious meetings; have spoken thousands of times on Bible subjects, to thousands of people; have received thousands of dollars; have had thousands of good hearty shakes of the hand with brethren in the Lord; have been saved from thousands of snares and temptations; have been benefited in various ways thousands and thousands of times, and have found thousands of precious truths in the Bible which I did not know were there before I searched it for myself. The Bible has been my light in darkness, my joy in sorrow, my song in affliction, my support in weariness, my guide in every perplexity. It is my chart, my compass, my beacon light. By it I discern the perils that surround me, and see the safe channel which leads to the celestial harbor. I love the Bible because it has done so much for me. I love it because it has done so much for my friends, I love it because it has done so much for the world. I love it, most of all, because it tells me of Jesus. His name is the golden thread that runs through all its sacred pages.

> " Wonderful things in the Bible I see—
> This is the dearest that Jesus loves me."

Yes, Jesus loves me, and you, and all mankind. The object of his coming into this world was to seek and to save that which was lost. This we shall see as we proceed to investigate some of the wonderful truths of the Holy volume. The Psalmist not only says, "Thy testimonies are wonderful," but he also says, "The entrance of thy words giveth light." I can testify to the truthfulness of this: Once I was in complete darkness, but by a careful study of the Scriptures, I find among other things the following

RAYS OF LIGHT.

I. *Mankind by nature are sinners, and need a Saviour.* This is very plain, yet many do not understand it. By turning back to the first part of Genesis we see how things were in the beginning. Here we find that all things were *originally* created very good. There was no sin, no curse, no death. All was beautiful as far as the eye could see or the imagination roam. The earth presented one scene of transcendent loveliness. The morning stars sang together, and all the sons of God shouted for joy. Man was placed in Eden, with the prospect of subduing the earth and having dominion over it. He possessed a mind capable of obeying or of disobeying his Creator. He was not a mere machine, only acting as he was acted upon. He was free to choose for himself. Two courses were placed before him—right and wrong. Which did he choose? Adam by transgression fell. What was the result? The ground was cursed. Sorrow and death came into the world. "By one man sin entered into the world and death by sin." What effect had this sin upon the human race? "All have sinned and come short of the glory of God." Rom. 3. 23. "All we, like sheep, have gone astray; We have turned every one to his own way." Isa. 53. 6.

II. *God loved the world in its fallen condition, and promised a Saviour.* It would have been just and right, after

man had sinned if his Creator had exe-
cuted the penalty of His law immediately
upon him. It was a great offense which
Adam had committed, and the consequences of that transgression were to be
terribly effective upon the human family.
But in the bosom of the Eternal there
was a fountain of grace. Notwithstanding the gates of Eden were closed, the
tree of life guarded, the earth cursed,
and man's existence limited, yet, even in
this we see marks of the Divine compassion. The earth was still full of His
riches. Long life was still vouchsafed
to man. Each rising and setting sun,
each returning harvest gave token of the
Creator's goodness. But the greatest
expression of His grace was seen in
the promise of a Saviour. Looking out
through blinding tears Adam and Eve
caught glimpses of one brilliant star—
it was the star of hope. "The seed of the
woman shall bruise the serpent's head."
Gen. 3. 15.

III. *At the appointed time the prom-*

ised Saviour appeared. From the day his coming was first announced amid the retreating glories of Eden, he had been spoken of in promise, shadowed forth in types, sung of by poets, and predicted by prophets, until one dark night a bright angel came down from Heaven and said to the Shepherds of Bethlehem, " Fear not ; for behold, I bring you good tidings of great joy, which shall be to all people. For unto you is born this day in the city of David a Saviour, which is Christ the Lord. And this shall be a sign unto you: Ye shall find the babe wrapped in swaddling clothes, lying in a manger." Luke 2. 11, 12. The appointed time had arrived. He could not have come before, he could not have come later. All of God's plans and purposes are in perfect time and order. " When the fulness of time was come, God sent forth His Son, made of a woman, made under the law, to redeem them that were under the law, that we might receive the adoption of sons." Gal. 4. 4.

29*

IV.　*He was just such a Saviour as man needed.*　Had he been anything else than what he was, he would not have been suited to our condition.　Man was not only lost in sin, but without strength—unable to save himself.　He needed one who could sympathize with him, and one who had power to deliver him.　This, Jesus could do, for he was both a human and a divine Saviour.　He was the Son of God, and the Son of man.　Like us, He was born of a woman.　He became one with us.　He had a body like our own.　Like us, He ate and drank, and rested and slept.　Like us, He sorrowed, and wept, and felt.　Like us, He was often hungry, and thirsty, and faint, and weary.　Like us, was He in all things, sin only excepted.　"For verily He took not on Him the nature of angels; but He took on Him the seed of Abraham.　Wherefore in all things it behoved Him to be made like unto His brethren, that He might be a merciful and faithful high priest in things pertaining to God, to make reconciliation for the sins of the people. For in that He himself hath suffered being tempted, He is able to succor them that are tempted." Heb. 2. 17, 18.

V. *He opened the way by which man could be reconciled to God.* Sin had raised a barrier between men and their heavenly Father. Jesus came to take that barrier out of the way. Sin had driven man away from God. Jesus came to bring man back to God. The law had been broken. Jesus kept the law. The law was given by Moses, but grace and truth came by Jesus Christ. The law had no claim on Jesus, for he kept it perfectly, yet he suffered its penalty to redeem those who had broken it, and were unable to redeem themselves. God is satisfied with the death of His Son. He now calls upon men to cease their rebellion, and be reconciled to Him. " All things are of God, who hath re-conciled us to himself by Jesus Christ, and hath given unto us the ministry of

reconciliation; to wit: that God was in
Christ reconciling the world unto himself, not imputing their trespasses unto
them: and hath committed unto us the
word of reconciliation. Now then we
are ambassadors for Christ, as though
God did beseech you by us: we pray
you in Christ's stead, be ye reconciled
to God. For he hath made him to be
sin for us who know no sin; that we
might be made the righteousness of God
in Him."   2 Cor. 6. 19, 20, 21.

VI. *He has provided salvation for all
who will ask for it?* The gospel was
first offered to the Jews because they
were God's peculiar people. Some from
amongst them received it, but not all.
The death of Jesus broke down the middle wall of partition between Jews and
Gentiles. Salvation is now offered free
to all classes. The Saviour's first commission to his disciples was "Go ye
to the lost sheep of the house of Israel."
His last commission was "Go ye into
all the world, and preach the gospel to

every creature, he that believeth, and is baptized shall be saved." God is no respector of persons. The fountain of mercy that was opened on Calvary sends its streams through all nations. Whosoever will, let him come and partake of the water of life freely. Whether young or old, rich or poor, it matters not. All can have salvation who will ask for it in faith "For it shall come to pass, that whosoever shall call on the name of the Lord shall be saved.—Acts ii. 21.

VII. *He saves his people from their sins in the present tense.* I believe in a present salvation. Jesus came into this world to save sinners. He did not come to save them *in* their sins, but *from* their sins. His name indicated the work he was to perform. " Thou shalt call his name Jesus: for he shall save his people from their sins." He saved many when he was on earth. To the man sick with the palsy he said " Son, thy sins are forgiven thee." To the woman bowed in penitence at his feet he said "Thy faith hath saved thee, go in peace and sin no more." He saves to-day. All who trust in him know what present salvation means. His people do not walk in darkness. They have passed from death unto life. He is exalted as a Prince and a Saviour, to give repentance and remission of sins to all that will call upon him. From his throne he sends down a pardon here and there to all who truly believe. The way is simple. It is only to look and live. "Look unto me all ye ends of the earth and be ye saved." Isa. xlv. 22.

VIII. *The object of his death was to redeem to himself a holy people.*—As it is said "without holiness no man shall see the Lord." So it is said, "without shedding of blood there is no remission." One is dependent on the other. There can be no holiness without remission of sins, and there can be no remission of sins except through faith in the blood of Christ. The way to the crown is by the cross. It is the blood that maketh atonement. Jesus died the just for the unjust, that he might bring us to God. His blood can cleanse from all sin, and purge the conscience from dead works to serve the living and true God. It is in Him that " we have redemption through his blood, even the forgiveness of sins, according to the riches of his grace." " And you, that were some time alienated and enemies in your mind by wicked works, yet now hath he reconciled. In the body of his flesh through death, to present you *holy* and *unblameable* and *unreprovable in his sight.*" Col. i. 21, 22.

IX. *He gives the Holy Spirit to every true believer.* When an individual is forgiven of his sins, the next thing for him to look for is the gift of the spirit. The Saviour promised this to his disciples before he went away. " Tarry," said he, " in Jerusalem, until ye be endued with power from on high." On the day of Pentecost, this spirit came down with wonderful power. The disciples were filled with it. It has been in the world ever since, convincing men of sin, of righteousness, and of a judgment to come. This spirit dwells in believer, leads them into truth, comforts their hearts, and bears witness with their spirit, that they are the children of God. We are commanded to be "filled with the spirit," to "walk in the spirit," to "grieve not the spirit."   Paul once asked certain individuals if they had "received the holy spirit since they believed." This is an important question. How is it with us? Have we received the spirit? "Now, if any man have not the spirit of Christ he is none of his." Rom. viii. 9.

X. His people, though holy, are not exempt from sorrow, trouble or death. The disciple cannot expect to be greater than his Lord. If He was a man of sorrows, and acquainted with grief," it is no wonder if his followers have a portion of the same experience. None can escape affliction. The best and holiest people are sometimes the greatest sufferers. Man that is born of a woman is of few days, and full of trouble. He cometh forth like a flower, and is cut down: he fleeth also as a shadow, and continueth not." All human beings are mortal, and though some may possess pure hearts, yet they are subject to affliction, and to death like others. The sentence which consigns man to dust has not yet been revoked. The pure and good of all ages have died. Even David, the sweet singer of Israel—the man after God's own heart—"is not ascended into Heaven, but is both dead and buried, and his sepulchre is with us unto this day." Acts 2. 29, 34.

XI. *The resurrection of Christ shed light on the grave, and opened the way to a future life.* Though Christians are subject to death, they have a glorious hope of immortality. From the rock hewn tomb of Joseph of Arimathea, we see and trace a single brilliant ray of light and hope. If the dead Christ is alive, then there is a way out of death. It was in the morning early that the women came to the sepulchre, and lo! they found the stone rolled away and an angel sitting upon it, which said unto them, "Fear not: I know that ye seek Jesus, which was crucified. He is not here; for he is risen, as he said. Come see the place where the Lord lay. And go quickly and tell his disciples that he is risen from the dead." Christ is alive. What joyful news. He showed himself to his disciples by many infallible proofs, being seen of them forty days, and speak· ing of things pertaining to the kingdom of God. "So then after the Lord had spoken these things, He was received up into Heaven, and sat on the right hand of God." Mark 16. 19.

XII. *He will come back again from Heaven to this world.* Not forever will He remain away. He cannot be always separated from his people. He went up there to intercede, and to prepare mansions for those who love Him. But

He will come again. So He said to His disciples before He left them. "Let not your heart be troubled: ye believe in God, believe also in me. In my Father's house are many mansions; if it were not so, I would have told you. I go to prepare a place for you. And if I go and prepare a place for you I will come again, and receive you unto my-self; that where I am there ye may be also." And as he departed and went up into Heaven, two angels in white apparel, stood by the disciples, which also said, "Ye men of Galilee, why stand ye gazing up into Heaven? this same Jesus, which is taken up from you into Heaven, shall so come in like man-ner as ye have seen Him go into Heaven." Acts 1. 11.

XIII. *He will come personally, visi-bly, with His holy angels, amid clouds of glory.* Not in a disembodied, invisible, spiritual form will He return, but the "same Jesus" in "like manner" as he went away. It was a real Christ that

died, it was a real Christ that was buried,
it was a real Christ that rose from the
dead and ascended into Heaven. It
will be a real Christ that returns to this
earth. He went up to Heaven with a
body, He will come back with the same
body. He was seen when He went up,
He will be seen when He comes back.
He had angels for His guards and attendants when on earth, He will have
angel escorts and attendants when He
returns. He went up amid clouds of
glory, He will come back with the same.
" When the Son of man shall come in
His glory and all the holy angels with
Him, then shall He sit upon the throne
of His glory."

" Behold, He cometh with clouds, and
every eye shall see Him." Rev. 1. 7.

XIV. *His coming will be sudden, and
unexpected by the world.* The prophecies will be fulfilled, and signs in Heaven
and earth will betoken His coming near,
but the unbelieving will not heed them.
There will be scoffers in the last days,

saying, "Where is the promise of His coming." The professed church will be in a corrupt and fearfully backslidden condition. Ministers will eat and drink with the drunken, smite their fellow servants, and say in their hearts, "My Lord delayeth His coming." Love will wax cold, and iniquity abound. Crime will be on the increase, and distress and perplexity will prevail. "As it was in the days of Noah, when they were eating, and drinking, marrying and giving in marriage, and knew not until the flood came, and took them all away; So shall also the coming of the Son of man be." Take heed, for "as a snare shall it come on all them that dwell on the face of the whole earth." Luke 21. 35.

XV. *His coming is the hope of His people, and will be desired and looked for, by those who truly love Him.* While the world is in darkness and unbelief, the true Christian will be searching the Scriptures, discerning the signs of the times, and watching for his Saviour to

come. "But ye brethren are not in darkness that that day should overtake you
as a thief." "For the grace of God that
bringeth salvation hath appeared to all
men. Teaching us that, denying ungod-
liness and worldly lusts, we should live
soberly, righteously and Godly in this
present world; Looking for that blessed
hope and the glorious appearing of the
great God and our Saviour Jesus Christ."
Titus 2. 11–13.

Paul looked forward to this day as
the time when he would receive his reward, and he anticipated a crown for all
who loved the appearing of his Master.
"I have fought a good fight, I have finished my course, I have kept the faith.
Henceforth there is laid up for me a
crown of righteousness, which the Lord,
the righteous Judge, shall give me at
that day; and not to me only, but unto
all them also that love his appearing."
2 Tim. 4. 7, 8.

XVI. *His coming will be the signal
for the resurrection of the dead.* Now

let us stick to the Bible if it knocks all our preconceived opinions overboard It is the word of God, that we want to prove every point.   There is to be a res-urrection of the dead of both classes, the righteous and the wicked. " But this I confess unto thee, that after the way which they call heresy, so worship I the God of my fathers, believing all things which are written in the law and in the prophets.   And have hope toward God which they themselves also allow, that there shall be a resurrection of the dead, both of the just and unjust."   Acts 24. 14, 15. " Marvel not at this; for the hour is coming in the which all that are in the graves shall hear his voice and shall come forth, they that have done good unto the resurrection of life, and they that have done evil unto the resur-rection of condemnation."   John 5. 28, 29. " I charge thee therefore before God, and the Lord Jesus Christ, who shall judge the quick and the dead at his *ap-pearing* and *kingdom.*"   2 Tim. 4. 1.

XVII. *This will be the time for the judgment of the whole world.* Men cannot be judged until they are raised, so the judgment follows the resurrection of the dead. "God shall bring every work into judgment with every secret thing, whether it be good or bad." "I saw in the night visions, and, behold, One like the Son of man came with the clouds of Heaven. A fiery stream issued and came forth from before him; thousand thousands ministered unto him, and ten thousand times ten thousand stood before him; the judgment was set and the books were opened." Dan. 7. 10. "When the Son of man shall come in His glory and all the holy angels with Him, then shall He sit upon the throne of His glory. And before Him shall be gathered all nations; and He shall separate them one from another, as a shepherd divideth his sheep from the goats." Matt. 25. 31, 32. "And the sea gave up the dead which were in it; and death and hell delivered up the dead which were in them; and they were judged every man according to their works." Rev. 20. 13.

XVIII. *He will then save his people with an everlasting salvation.* Believers are saved *now* from sin by faith; *then* they will be saved finally, and completely, with an everlasting salvation. Unto them that look for him shall he appear the second time without sin unto salvation. Some will be living when he appears. " Behold, I show you a mystery: we shall not all sleep, but we shall all be changed. In a moment, in the twinkling of an eye, at the last trump: for the trumpet shall sound, and the dead shall be raised incorruptible, and we shall be changed. For this corruptible must put on incorruption, and this mortal must put on immortality. So when this corruptible shall have put on incorruption, and this mortal shall have put on immortality, then shall be brought to pass the saying that is written: Death is swallowed up in victory, O death, where is thy sting? O grave, where is thy victory? Thanks be to God, which giveth us the victory through our Lord Jesus Christ." 1 Cor. 15. 51–57.

XIX. *The wicked will then be cast off at the left hand and forever destroyed.* Sin is not to be continued forever. The wages of sin is death. Sinners must be punished. What shall be the end of those who reject the offers of mercy, and obey not the gospel? "The Lord Jesus Christ shall be revealed from Heaven with His mighty angels, in flaming fire, taking vengeance on those who know not God, and that obey not the gospel. Who shall be punished with everlasting destruction from the presence of the Lord, and from the glory of His power; when He shall come to be glorified in His saints, and to be admired in all them that believe." 2 Thess. 1. 7, 8, 9. He shall say to those on his left hand, "Depart from me, ye cursed, into everlasting fire, prepared for the devil and his angels." Sodom and Gomorrah are set forth as examples to the ungodly suffering the vengeance of eternal fire. "Death and hell were cast into the lake of fire." This is the second death. And whosoever was not found written in the book of life was cast into the lake of fire." Rev. 20. 14, 15.

XX. *Then the earth will be purified by fire and restored to its former beauty and loveliness.* The earth will be purified, cleansed, all wickedness destroyed out of it, the curse removed, and then restored to more than its Eden like glory. Jesus was received up into Heaven, there to remain, until the times of restitution of all things, which God hath spoken by the mouth of the holy prophets since the world began. Acts 3. 21. "The day of the Lord will come as a thief in the night; in the which the Heavens shall pass away with a great noise, and the elements shall melt with a fervent heat, the earth also, and the works that are therein shall be burned up. Seeing then that all these things shall be dissolved, what manner of per-

sons ought ye to be in all holy conversation and godliness. Looking for and
hastening unto the coming of the day of
God, wherein the Heavens being on fire
shall be dissolved, and the elements shall
melt with fervent heat. *Nevertheless we,
according to His promise, look for new
Heavens and a new earth, wherein dwelleth righteousness.*" 2 Pet. 3. 10–13.

XXI. *The Saviour will then establish
his kingdom on the renewed earth and
with his saints reign forever and ever.*
Having raised the dead, judged the
world, saved his people, destroyed the
wicked, purified and restored the earth,
He now establishes His kingdom, and
begins His everlasting reign. "There
was given Him dominion, and glory, and
a kingdom, that all people, nations and
languages, should serve Him : His dominion is an everlasting dominion, which
shall not pass away, and His kingdom
that which shall not be destroyed. Dan.
7. 14." And the seventh angel sounded,
and there were great voices in Heaven,

saying, "The kingdoms of this world are become the kingdoms of our Lord and of His Christ; and He shall reign forever and ever." Rev. 11. 15. "And the kingdom and dominion, and the greatness of the kingdom *under* the whole Heaven, shall be given to the people of the saints of the most High, whose kingdom is an everlasting kingdom, and all dominions shall serve and obey Him." Dan. 7. 27. Paradise is now restored. The dominion lost by the first Adam's transgression, is now restored by the second Adam, and *here*, with His redeemed family, will He reign in unparalleled glory forever and ever. How beautifully the Bible closes. "And I saw a new Heaven and and a new Earth; for the first Heaven and the first Earth were passed away; and there was no more sea. And I, John, saw the Holy City, new Jerusalem, coming down from God out of Heaven, prepared as a bride adorned for her husband. And I heard a great voice out of Heaven saying, Behold the Tabernacle

of God is with men, and He will dwell
with them, and they shall be His people, and God himself shall be with them
and be their God.   And God shall wipe
away all tears from their eyes; and there
shall be no more death, neither sorrow
nor crying, neither shall there be any
more pain; for the former things are
passed away.   And He that sat on the
throne said, *Behold I make all things
new.*" Rev. 21. 1–7.   Are not these glorious promises?   I have quoted them
from the Bible.   What other book tells
of *such* a Saviour and presents *such* a
hope? There is none like it.   As Christ
is the King of kings, so the Bible is the
King of books.   It is more precious than
gold.   O yes,—

" This holy book I'd rather own,
    Than all the gold and gems
That e'er in monarch's coffers shone,
    Than all their diadems.

Nay, were the seas one chrysolite,
    The earth one golden ball,
And diamonds all the stars of night,
    This book was worth them all.

Ah, no! the soul ne'er found relief
  In glittering hoards of wealth;
Gems dazzle not the eye of grief;
  Gold cannot purchase health.

But here a blessed balm appears
  To heal the deepest woe;
And those who read this book in tears,
Their tears shall cease to flow."